WHAT THE DICKENS!

Other books by Jane Louise Curry

THE GREAT FLOOD MYSTERY

THE LOTUS CUP

BACK IN THE BEFORETIME:
TALES OF THE CALIFORNIA INDIANS
Illustrated by James Watts

ME, MYSELF, AND I

LITTLE LITTLE SISTER
Illustrated by Erik Blegvad

THE BIG SMITH SNATCH

(MARGARET K. McELDERRY BOOKS)

WHAT THE DICKENS!

Jane Louise Curry

Margaret K. McElderry Books
New York

Maxwell Macmillan Canada
Toronto

Maxwell Macmillan International
New York Oxford Singapore Sydney

With apologies to Ada, Leon, and Mr. Dickens!

Margaret K. McElderry Books
Macmillan Publishing Company
866 Third Avenue
New York, NY 10022

Maxwell Macmillan Canada, Inc.
1200 Eglinton Avenue East
Suite 200
Don Mills, Ontario M3C 3N1

Macmillan Publishing Company is part of the Maxwell Communication Group of
Companies.

First edition
Printed in the United States of America
10 9 8 7 6 5 4 3 2 1
Designed by Nancy B. Williams

Library of Congress Cataloging-in-Publication Data
Curry, Jane Louise.
What the Dickens! / Jane Louise Curry.
p.   cm.
Summary: In 1842, eleven-year-old twins, whose father runs a boat
on the Juniata Canal in Pennsylvania, learn of a Harrisburg
bookseller's plan to steal Charles Dickens's newly finished novel
while Dickens himself is touring the U.S.
ISBN 0-689-50524-8
[1. Twins—Fiction. 2. Canals—Pennsylvania—Fiction. 3. Dickens,
Charles, 1812–1870—Fiction.]   I. Title.
PZ7.C936Wh 1991   [Fic]—dc20   90-26864

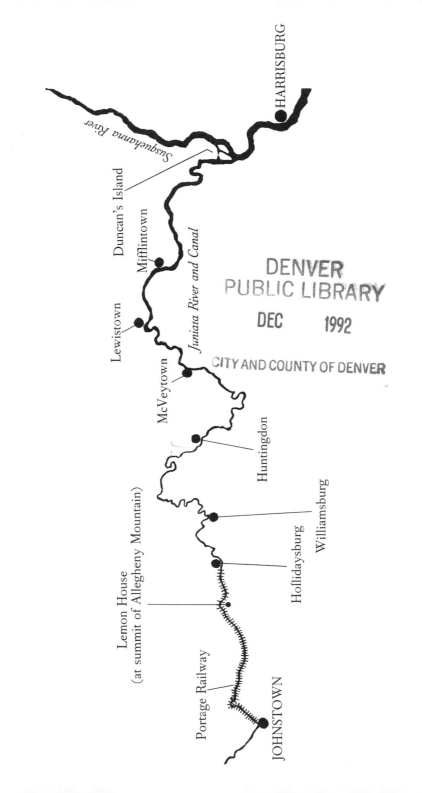

HARRISBURG

Susquehanna River

Duncan's Island

Mifflintown

Juniata River and Canal

Lewistown

McVeytown

Huntingdon

Williamsburg

Hollidaysburg

Lemon House
(at summit of Allegheny Mountain)

Portage Railway

JOHNSTOWN

1

Thursday, March 24th, 1842

"Where the dad-blasted dickens *is* that gal?" Captain Dobbs, skipper of the canal boat *Betty D.*, bellowed into the wind.

Cherry Dobbs, down in the tiny family cabin, did not hear—but not because of the wind, or the rain drumming on the cabin roof. In her imagination she was a thousand miles west of Pennsylvania and the Susquehanna Canal. Her apron pocket was mended, and she had stuck the needle under her coat collar, wound the long tail of thread around it, and fetched her beautiful store-bought notebook from the corner cupboard. Then, hunched over the notebook on the edge of a lower bunk bed, she had set to work. Twice she crossed out a word and, frowning, wrote in another. In the middle of the next sentence she stopped to chew on the end of her pencil as she wavered over the spellings of *spear* and *cruel.*

The notebook on Cherry's lap was her prize possession—

a combined birthday and Christmas gift that Captain Dobbs had bought in a fancy shop in Harrisburg. Before the notebook, she had had to make do with stitched-together letter paper.

The new book had a stiff cover, almost like a real book. Cherry had penciled her name in curlicue letters on the front of the plain blue cover. Between its plain blue covers, however, there was nothing plain about the book. The title, *The Indian Maid's Revenge,* was spelled out in fancy capitals on the first page, with her name, Charity Ann Dobbs, underneath. More than half of the pages were already filled with the noise and color of the stories that teemed inside Cherry's head—stories of heroes and villains and hair-raising dangers. Cherry was sure that when her book was finished it would be every bit as exciting as any printed book bound in fancy embossed covers. When she imagined *The Indian Maid's Revenge* on the New Books table at Mr. Greenleaf's book shop in Harrisburg, she saw it in just such a cover, embossed in red and blue with handsome gold lettering.

Cherry chewed on a fingernail as she reread the new paragraph once more.

The evil~~l~~ trapper gave a ~~shreek~~ shriek of fear as Summer Moons warning arrow struck the tree he skullk'd behind. Brandishing her shining ~~speer~~ spear, she leeped from the ledge to stand between the bloodthristy villian and his helpless ~~pray~~ prey. Brave-Heart the Beever, his paw clunch'd in the trap's ~~erewel~~ cruel jaws—

She scowled. Was *clunched* a real word—or had she just that minute invented it by sticking *clenched* and *crunched* together? Her mother frowned at made-up words, but Cherry decided that she liked this one. Both *clench* and *crunch* worked fine with *jaws*. She read on.

Up on deck in the rain, Captain Dobbs let go the canalboat's tiller for half a moment to cup his hands and call down to Cherry's twin, Sam, who was hard at work belowdecks with the bilge pump. Sam's head popped up through the hatchway at his father's feet.

"Where's that sis of yours creept off to?" Captain Dobbs called over the drumming of the rain. "Rockville Lock's comin' up soon, dang it. It's past time she took over the drivin'. Young Darsie's been out in the rain for near a mile now. That's too far in the mud for such a little feller."

Eleven-year-old Sam leaned his head back and lifted the floppy hat brim that kept the rain out of his eyes. "Last I saw, she was still down in the cabin, Pap," he yelled back.

"What the blazes is she fussin' at down there?"

Sam grinned. "I dunno. Washin' her face and tyin' on a pink ribbon for the big city, mebbe."

"Hah! She'll be mud from stem to stern 'fore she gets there," Captain Dobbs growled. He cupped his hands again, and gave a loud *"Halloo!"* along the canal towpath to six-year-old Darsie.

Darsie trudged along half hidden under his oilskin rain cape, beside Bell, the big chestnut gelding, whose back was

3

covered by a canvas rain cape of his own. Darsie was proud to take his turn as driver, but it was hard work in the rain. His feet slipped and dragged in the mud, and the wet reins were heavy and cold in his too-small hands. Other six-year-old drivers on the Juniata and Susquehanna canals might ride their towhorses like some of the big boys, but not Darsie. A horse and rider could be snatched into the water if a too-taut towrope snagged on the bottom of a passing boat. Not Darsie. He meant to be the second-best canal man in the world one day—after his pap. That meant keeping on Bell's off side and doing everything exactly right. Darsie tried to do everything right even when he was tired enough to curl up and go to sleep right in the middle of the muddy towpath.

"Ho, Darsie!" Captain Dobbs bellowed again. "Ease off, boy. Cherry's comin' out. Rockville Lock's just a piece up ahead." He beckoned to Sam to come up on deck and take the tiller.

Sam grinned through the rain that poured from his hat brim. "I thought we were goin' to stop before the lock," he yelled. He grasped the arm of the wooden tiller that steered the boat. "Ain't we puttin' Grinny out on the towpath, too? Cherry says you mean to let her drive both horses into Harrisburg, like what's-her-name, that olden-days warrior queen who drove around in a two-wheel chariot."

"Queen Boo-dicka? Hah!" Captain Dobbs snorted. "Don't Cherry wish! As if I'd use two horses headin' down easy water into a trafficky canal basin. You ought to know better'n to pay any mind to your sis's moonshine. She dreams it up by the bucketful." He raised the boat's old tin trumpet and blew a *too-too-too-it!* of four short toots to warn the lockkeeper ahead that the *Betty D.* was coming. Then he cupped his hands to roar once more toward the cabin steps.

"Cherry, gal! Shake a leg and git up here!"

Down below, Cherry jumped at the trumpet's bleat.

"Oh, fuzzbuzz!" She straightened too quickly and banged her head against the upper bunk. "Ouch!"

Rubbing the top of her head, Cherry slipped the book under the folded blanket at the foot of her own bed and pulled on her rain cape. Then she darted through the galley and up the gangway to the *Betty D.*'s rear deck. The rain had begun to slack off a little.

"I'm sorry, Pap! I clean forgot it was my turn. Old Brave-Heart's got his paw caught in a trap, you see, and—"

"Charity Ann Dobbs!"

This time Captain Dobbs's roar had a real snap to it, a sternness that the children did not often hear. Cherry hastily pulled up her work apron and skirt in front and back to tuck them into her sash, and climbed the six steps to the cabin roof. There she snatched up the long pole that lay along the roof-deck's edge, backed up, took a run, and leaped. The pole slipped a little on the wet roof, but Cherry's vault still carried her across the six feet of water to the towpath.

She landed neatly enough, but the little stagger as she touched the ground turned into a sideways slither in the mud. Furious, she picked herself up and bent to waggle her hands

5

clean in the water of the canal. Clumsy! Summer Moon would never stagger when she landed after a leap, and *never* slipped. Not in the wildest windstorm or—

Darsie suddenly let out a hoarse cry and there was no time to think of Summer Moon.

"Low bridge!" Darsie croaked again.

Cherry ran to snatch Bell's reins from her little brother. She gave him a push. "Hurry! You'll miss it if you don't hustle!"

Little Darsie broke into a stiff-legged, slithery run. At the crest of the bridge he had barely time to climb onto the low parapet on the far side. The *Betty D.*, with Sam at the tiller, was already nosing out from under it. Captain Dobbs, stretched out flat on the roof while the boat slid under the bridge, scrambled up just in time to catch Darsie as he jumped.

"L-o-o-ck R-e-a-d-y?" Captain Dobbs bellowed ahead as he set Darsie down.

The lockkeeper's answer, *"R-e-a-d-y!"* came back dimly through the rain. Captain Dobbs turned to shout at Cherry. "Whoa up there, gal! I don't see anybody racin' us for the lock."

"Hoa there, whoa-a-bit!" Cherry called glumly. She pulled back on Bell's reins. Cherry was not one to be glum for long, though, even with her stockings muddy to the knees. If there was no excitement to be had on the approach to Rockville Lock, adventures aplenty waited for her at the booksellers' shops in Harrisburg. On this trip it was Cherry's turn to choose a new book for the Dobbs family to read to one another in the story hour after supper, back home with Mrs. Dobbs and Merry and Baby Ellen.

Cherry had not made up her mind what book to buy. Not knowing was half the pleasure. The story would have to have danger and escapes, and bravery, and midnight skulkings and thievery or robbery. Perhaps even murder. Everything had to come out all right in the end, too. Mr. Walter Scott's *Castle Dangerous,* which the Dobbses had just finished, had been fine, but not as stirring as his *Rob Roy. The Pirate* might be good. Or Captain Marryat's new sea story, *Masterman Ready.* Cherry frowned. Darsie and Pap would like that. They liked any story that had to do with boats and water. Cherry preferred stories with dry land and horses. And olden times. Sam liked all sorts.

"Sla-a-a-ack!" Captain Dobbs called.

The captain's warning boomed through Cherry's daydream like a cannonball. She gave a jerk of the reins, but Bell, from long habit, was already slowing to a stop. As soon as the towrope dropped slackly into the water, Cherry unhitched it from the harness ring. Sam hauled the rope aboard the *Betty D.* as the long, narrow boat slid into the lock and Mr. Hatter, the lockkeeper, shut the upstream gates behind her. The *Betty D.* eased to a stop inches from the downstream gates.

"Snub 'er!" Captain Dobbs called.

Cherry bade Bell, "Stand!" Darting to the lockside, she and Mr. Hatter snubbed the *Betty D.*'s mooring rope around the forward stone bollard. Then Mr. Hatter sloshed over to open the downstream sluice. As the water level in the lock fell, Captain Dobbs kept a sharp lookout over the side for fear the *Betty D.* should scrape against the lock's stone wall. Each time he signaled, Cherry and Mr. Hatter eased off a bit on the rope. Once the water was at the level of the downstream stretch of canal, Mr. Hatter trotted along to open the gates.

"Gee-up for Harrisburg!" Cherry sang out to Bell when the towrope was once again hitched up to the harness. She gave Bell's rump a slap with the reins and he stepped out with a toss of his head that made the bells on his harness jingle merrily. He had been hard at work for five hours, but his step was almost frisky. Perhaps Cherry's excitement was catching.

More likely, Bell knew very well that two miles beyond Rockville Lock lay a canal basin and an extra few hours or even a day of rest.

The two-mile journey down to Harrisburg was too busy with "packets," as the passenger boats were called, and freight boats passing in both directions for Cherry to fret about not being allowed to drive Bell faster. Her excitement began to fizz again as the *Betty D.* slid under the Herr Street bridge. The weighlocks at the entrance to the canal basin lay dead ahead!

The line of boats ahead of the Dobbses was longer than usual. Docking seemed to take forever, but at last the *Betty D.* nudged up against the wharf of the Boatmen's Line.

Cherry whipped off her work apron and pitched it down the cabin steps. "May I go now, Pap? May I?"

"Soon as Bell's stowed in the stable and has his feed," Captain Dobbs answered from the stern of the boat. "You'll have time aplenty, gal. I'll come 'round the bookshops near onto closing time with your dollar. That'll leave you the best part of an hour to pick your book." With a bound, he leaped to the wharf and tied fast the aft rope. Then he strode off toward the collector's office. The canal charges—three cents a mile for each ton of crockery the *Betty D.* carried—had to be paid before he could go to the warehouse to arrange for the unloading of the three dozen barrels of china from Ohio, and to sign up for a return cargo.

Little Darsie watched as Sam and Cherry coaxed big Bell, one hoof at a time, down the awkward step from the wharf to the deck. Sam, pulling on Bell's reins, grinned to see Cherry pushing hard with both hands against the horse's big hindquarters. Bell's wet tail swished across her face.

"Pffoo!" Cherry wrinkled her nose and stuck out her tongue at the taste of horse hair. "I'm no fly, you old dobbin. That stung!"

"He doesn't feel you shovin' at him any more'n if you was a fly walkin' 'round on his rump," Sam said. "There! He's all right now. I'll get him down the ramp into his stall and give him his oats. You go along and pick us a good story."

"One with boats!" Darsie yelled as Cherry raced down the wharf and off toward the bridge over the weighlocks.

Once across the canal, Cherry, clutching her rain cape tight around her, ran all the way along Canal Street to Market Street, jumping puddles as she went. Passing the United States Hotel, she slowed. Suddenly shy, she pushed a straggly curl back under her hood and brushed at her skirt while she pretended to read a poster announcing the first canal trip by the speedy new Peerless Packet. A quick look at her reflection in a shopwindow showed a wide smear on her cheek, and she tried to use the hem of her cape, and then the back of her hand, to rub it off. Seeing citified ladies in deep-brimmed bonnets, flared skirts, and puff-shouldered coats below their umbrellas made her feel miserably wet and muddy. She forgot all about the spick-and-span ladies, though, once she caught sight of the sign, shaped like a gold quill pen, that hung in front of D. P. GREENLEAF, BOOKSELLER AND PRINTER. Lamps shone behind the rain-streaked window with BOOKS lettered on it in gold. Cherry could see new books in neat stacks on the heavy, polished tables, books in handsome bindings, with brightly colored pictures. A small sign in the corner of the window read, MR. CHARLES DICKENS'S *PICK-WICK PAPERS*, NEWLY REPRINTED IN A DELUXE EDITION, TWO DOLLARS AND THIRTY-FIVE CENTS.

Two dollars and thirty-five cents? For a *book?* Why, two dollars and fifty cents would buy an iron stove!

Cherry dodged across the street between a brewer's cart and a heavy, old-fashioned carriage, and ended up in front of JASON GOODGE, PRINT SHOP. BOOKS NEW AND USED. Mr. Goodge did not have a handsome sign, and the books he printed had ugly covers and smudgy ink, but his prices were always lower than Greenleaf's or Pfalzgraff's, farther down the street. With luck, the dollar Captain Dobbs had promised Cherry might buy two or three good used books.

Dick Tapley, Mr. Goodge's gangly assistant, was up on a ladder flicking a feather duster over the highest shelves of books when Cherry pushed open the shop door. A cracked bell fixed to the door clattered in alarm.

"I swow!" Young Mr. Tapley's long face lit up with a smile. The smile was a rusty, not-much-used one, but it was still a great improvement. Mr. Tapley was tall and stoop-shouldered, with stringy black hair. In his worn black suit he looked like an apprentice undertaker.

Mr. Tapley clattered down the ladder backward. "I declare, it's Miss Dobbs again, so soon!" He threaded his way among the book tables toward the door and made her an awkward bow. "Have the Dobbses finished *Castle Dangerous* already?"

Cherry blushed as she nodded. She felt quite grown up at being bowed to, and gave a jerky little bob that she hoped was like the polite curtsies she had seen young ladies in lace mitts and straw bonnets give to older folks.

"Yessir, and it was a right good one, like you said. Maybe not so good as *Ivanhoe,* but right good anyhow."

Cherry blushed again as a lady in a ribbon-silk bonnet and plum wool shawl stared at her and sniffed. A gentleman leaning on a silver-headed cane looked up as if he, too, were startled to hear such a loud voice in the quiet shop.

"Gosh Neds, I'm sorry!" Cherry whispered. "I'm so used to callin' 'Slack off!' or 'Low bridge!' or whatnot all day that sometimes I forget I'm indoors."

"Tush, Miss Dobbs, no need to hush. This ain't a library, you know."

Mr. Tapley spoke up bravely enough for the nearest customers to hear, but cast an anxious look over his shoulder at a door in the back of the shop that said PRIVATE on its frosted glass window. When the shop bell gave a sudden jangle, he jumped as if he had been stuck with a hatpin. The heads of everyone in the shop swiveled toward the front door.

The two men who entered and banged the shop door shut behind them looked almost as surprised as Mr. Tapley, whose eyebrows shot up like exclamation points. One man was short and bowlegged, the other tall and broad shouldered. Both were dressed roughly and could have used a week's soak in a bathtub and a good scrub with a stiff brush and laundry soap. The tallish one doffed his moth-eaten beaver hat with the crooked turkey tail feather stuck in its band, and gaped at the book-laden tables.

"I'll be a ringtail turkey cock, ef they ain't got one of ever book that ever was! Jes' *lookit,* Sim."

"Keep yer flap shut," the shorter man snapped as he looked around sharply. "We dint come in t' gawp." He glared at young Mr. Tapley and pulled his hat down so sharply that his ears stood out sideways under the brim. "If this here's Goodge's, where's Goodge?"

Mr. Tapley pointed wordlessly at the door marked PRIVATE. The small man, his tall shadow close at his heels, charged back through the book tables and barged right in without so much as a warning knock. Mr. Tapley drew in his breath sharply and hunched his shoulders. When no explosion followed, he let out a sigh of relief.

12

"Mr. Goodge must be in a right good mood. If *I* forget to knock, you can hear the ruckus all the way to the City Water Works."

Taking Cherry's elbow, he steered her to the nearest table and pointed at a stack of books bound in dark blue. They bore the title *Master Humphrey's Clock* embossed in black and gold.

"Now, this here's just the volume for the Dobbses. By Mr. Dickens. Two tales for the price of one, and fat enough to last even greedy readers a good long spell. It's fresh come from Philadelphia, where it was printed from the very first copy hot off the boat from London, England. Well, almost the first. Or here—here's our own Goodge's Cheap Edition of *Old St. Paul's,* Mr. Ainsworth's latest work. Only a dollar."

Cherry wrinkled her nose at the book's sour green cover. "Maybe. But I reckon I'll take a look in the cubbyhole first."

The bookshelf-lined cubbyhole next to Mr. Goodge's office at the back held an assortment of used books that were sometimes as cheap as five cents. Some were broken-backed, some coverless, and some foxed with rusty splotches from living in damp houses, but what did that matter? So long as no pages were missing, each told the same story as a dollar copy that still smelled of printer's ink.

Cherry always started with the bottom shelves, then with the help of the tall stool that stood in the corner, worked her way up to the ceiling. There was no lamp, and on so dark an afternoon only the titles on the bottom shelves could easily be seen. Cherry skimmed along them with a finger. Tattered primers and dusty collections of speeches and sermons were crowded in with a smattering of almanacs and atlases and books of travels with curious engravings. There were very few storybooks. Cherry supposed that other folks must, like the Dobbses, keep their storybooks to read over and over again until they fell apart. She did spy a *Pilgrim's Progress,* however, and a copy of Mr. Walter Scott's *The Fortunes of Nigel.* Mr. Scott's pages were all buckled up and stuck together as if they had fallen into a rain barrel and then been baked dry in an oven.

The volumes on the cubbyhole's middle shelves were as dull as ditchwater, every one of them. Cherry had to stand on tiptoe on the stool, peering to make out the titles on the top shelf. But there she found *Emmeline, the Orphan of the Castle,* one of the Rollo books, and a copy of Mr. Charles Dickens's *Nicholas Nickleby.* The price penciled inside the back cover of *Nicholas Nickleby* was twenty-five cents—a suspiciously good bargain for a book with a handsome cover. It had colored pictures, too.

As Cherry half expected, a closer look showed that a number of pages were missing. Once Captain Dobbs had brought home a twenty-five-cent *The Life and strange and surprising Adventures of Robinson Crusoe,* only to reach the exciting bit where Mr. Crusoe found the mysterious footprint on his deserted island—and find the next sixteen pages missing. The Dobbses had suffered in suspense for ten long days until the *Betty D.* called in at Harrisburg again and another copy could be found. Still . . .

As Cherry read through the chapter headings of *Nicholas Nickleby,* she began to fancy that she heard the murmur of voices, not from the outer shop but close at hand. She closed the book, keeping her finger at the place where she had stopped, and listened.

There *were* voices. Cherry could not make out what they were saying, but they seemed to come from somewhere close at hand. She stretched on tiptoe again to listen for a moment at the gap on the top shelf from which *Nicholas Nickleby* had come.

"... pack of foolishness ..." a small, gravelly voice was saying, followed by a deeper "Give'm a smart tap over the head an' jes' take it, I say."

Cherry's eyes widened. Very quietly, she slid *Nicholas Nickleby* in on top of the books on the second shelf down. Then she reached for the volume on the top shelf that had stood beside it. When she had removed it and three more, she saw where the sound came from. A faint pattern of light from the next room shone through a small iron ventilation grille in the shadows at the back of the shelf.

"Blithering idiots!" a third man's voice snapped. "You are not to lay a finger on him, or he an eye on you. Get that through your thick skulls!"

There was a gravelly grumble from the first voice, then the deeper voice rumbled, "'N this yere's him? He don't look like such a big bug. Purty as a petoony flower, ain't he?"

"Pah! That petunia's got ten times as much in his brainbox as you two daisies put together. So mind you step easy."

Cherry listened breathlessly. The three voices had to belong to Mister Goodge and his greasy-coated visitors. Surely something shady was afoot—but what?

"And you reckon it'll look purty much like this here?"

"I said so, didn't I? The dad-blasted thing might be any color. This name here—this's what you keep your eyes peeled for. Like as not, it'll be writ on the front."

"Mebbe you'd best write it down. Him and me ain't much of a hand at recollecting names," the gravelly voice grumbled.

Cherry stretched up on tiptoe again, but the view through the grille was disappointing. She could see nothing but the dingy office wall opposite. She considered stacking a large book or two on top of the stool, but it was dangerously wobbly already.

"Cherry!"

The stool shuddered as Cherry jumped in alarm. She craned around to see down, and spied her twin brother.

Cherry held a finger to her lips and made an anxious face.

"No. You come down," Sam's whisper was tight. "Quick. Pap's over at Boak's Tavern."

Cherry paused only a moment to push *Nicholas Nickleby* and *Emmeline* out of sight behind the other books on the top shelf. She might want to come back for them. Then she backed down the ladderlike rungs of the stool and sped out after Sam through the book tables.

Just as they reached the front door, the two scruffy men came out of Mr. Goodge's office, but Cherry did not see them. She had barely time to catch a glimpse of a startled Mr. Tapley raising his hand to her as if to say "But—". Then the door slammed at her back and she was racing up Market Street at Sam's heels.

Boak's Tavern!

There was not a minute to be lost. At that very moment their pap was probably standing drinks all around—with the *Betty D.*'s earnings, book dollar and all!

2

Darsie unexpectedly found himself alone on the *Betty D.* after the canal tariff had been paid to Mr. Eccles, the collector, the cargo of crockery unloaded, and the new cargo signed up for.

The report that Pap had brought back about their return cargo had been good news—to Darsie, at least. Their load of iron stoves was held up by a broken axle on the Keystone Iron Foundry's freight wagon. Because the rain had slacked off to a drizzle, to Darsie an extra hour or so meant time to take a look at the city.

He would have to go all on his lonesome, though. Sam had got himself all steamed up about something or other and slid off after Pap. The queer thing was, he had kept ducking behind dockmen or cargo barrels as if he didn't want Pap to see him. Darsie couldn't make out why. Their pap had nipped down into the *Betty D.*'s cabin for his fiddle and bow, and announced he'd be back before the iron stoves came. Then he hurried off with the fiddle and bow bundled up in a bit of old canvas tarpaulin. Nothing so odd in that. Captain Dobbs was the best fiddler between Lewistown and Lost Creek Ridge, maybe the best in the whole of the Juniata River valley. Folks were always asking him to "drop by for a nip of this and a bite of that, an' bring yer fiddle along." What cheerier way was there to fill up the tag end of a wet afternoon? Darsie found himself wishing he had followed Sam.

It might be too late for that, but it was not too late for a jaunt around the city. The central market, where he might find an orange to buy for Mam if they didn't cost too dear, was clear across town, but there were attractions aplenty close at hand. There were foundries and boat-building shops and livery stables and even a fire station with handsome, heavy-shouldered horses to pull the fire wagons. After boats, and the rest of the Dobbses, Darsie liked horses best in all creation.

First things first, though. Darsie's feet were cold in his too-big boots, so he tugged off his muddy stockings and pulled on a pair of cleaner, dry ones. Then he set off around the boat basin for the bridge over the canal.

From the bridge, State Street ran, broad and straight, smack up to the backside of the State Capitol Building. Darsie was sure the Capitol must be the biggest building in the world. Cherry called it "The Palace" because of the columns ringing its cupola, the tall arched gates that hitched it up to its side wings, and the pillared porches across the front. Sam always snorted and said all that was just fribble and that palaces were old-fangled. The Capitol, he said, was "the seat of democracy and the heart of the commonwealth." Pap liked to get Sam's goat by calling it "Old Baldy" because of the dome atop the cupola.

To Darsie, all that was just fuss about words. For him, the Capitol's main attraction was the stream of riders and carriages coming and going all day when the legislature was in session. Now and again there were rough-coated, sway-backed horses—old plugs pulling farm-style buckboards or hacks drawing cheap hired carriages—but trotting among them there were always beauties aplenty: gleaming grays with braided manes, silky blacks with polished hooves, handsome pacers with high-arched tails, and high-strung prancers with long, long legs.

Today, though, the rain had kept most travelers in their hotels and many other folks at home. Darsie found State Street half deserted. After slipping in for a look around the machine shop on the corner of Filbert Street, he hitched a ride on the back of a passing Harrisburg Cotton Mill wagon. When it reached the mill on Second Street, he dropped off and crossed to Fire Engine Company No. 2, to visit the horses. While he was there, a breathless boy came running in to report a fire in a shed on past the Baptist church and up Cranberry Alley.

To Darsie's delight, the fire fighters harnessed up their horses in a twinkling, boosted the breathless boy up beside the driver, threw open the big double doors, and whipped the engine out and down Second Street with bells clanging and the firehouse dog barking for joy. Best of all, in the moment before the engine sprang forward, the fireman hanging on at the back reached a hand down to swing Darsie up beside him.

The laundry-shed fire turned out to be no better than a bonfire, but the three-minute, bell-clanging, hoof-drumming engine dash through the drizzling rain was first-rate.

Afterward, too excited to go tamely back to the *Betty D.*, Darsie went exploring. From Cranberry Alley he made his way along Raspberry Alley to Walnut Street and a large new building, still empty, which truly *did* look a bit like a storybook castle with battlements and a turret on top. The lettering cut in the stonework over the stout front door spelled out DAUPHIN COUNTY PRISON, and though Darsie couldn't yet read, the bars on the windows made it easy to guess what the words said.

The rain had stopped. Lamplight shone from windows to brighten the afternoon as it darkened into evening. From the prison, instead of heading straight along Walnut to Canal Street, Darsie zigged and zagged. Of the passersby, not a one looked at him twice, for town folk, like country folk, were used to seeing children out on errands or trudging home from work. Darsie inspected the courthouse, watched the clerk at the telegraph office send a message, was treated to a short mug of ginger beer by the barman at a public house, climbed onto a barrel to peer in at the dark front window of a coach factory, and, drawn by a clatter of hooves and wheels, ran to see a huge coach pulled by four horses and driven by a man

21

in a short purple robe and a bearskin hat pull up in front of the splendid Eagle Hotel.

The four horses, all reddish chestnuts, stamped their hooves and shook their heads and harnesses. Their wet coats steamed and gleamed in the lamplight. But it was the driver Darsie stared at. His purple robe had a fur collar and was belted in with a parti-colored sash. His bearskin hat was tall and shaggy, his trousers gray, and his gloves a bright, light blue. Not even the canal showboat skipper, Sir Billy Mc-Ilhenny, was so splendid.

"Pretty nifty, ain't he?" piped up a voice from over Darsie's head. "He's my Uncle Nate. Here, grab aholt of this."

The speaker, a boy of about eight who sat with his legs dangling off the edge of the coach's roof, held out a gentleman's leather satchel, and dropped it into Darsie's outstretched arms. Leaving the heavier items to his uncle and the passenger who had shared the coachman's seat, the boy took hold of a loose baggage rope and lowered himself to the wet paving stones.

"That's his," the boy said, with a nod at the satchel and a jerk of his head toward the passenger above, who was handing down a small brassbound trunk. "He's the celebrated Buzz."

Darsie had never heard of the celebrated Mr. Buzz, and thought him nothing like as splendid as the coachman. The gentleman's greatcoat, though, was made of handsome dark fur, so unless he had trapped the animals and stitched the skins up into a coat himself, Mr. Buzz must be rich as well as famous. As Mr. Buzz climbed down, Darsie, hoping for a closer look, staggered around the back end of the coach with the heavy satchel. He set it down on the front step beside one of the columns that lined the hotel portico.

Five passengers had stepped down from inside the coach: two men and three women. An African in fawn-colored breeches, a striped waistcoat, and a green coat with shiny brass buttons came hurrying out from the hotel lobby with a large umbrella to keep the ladies' bonnets safe from any last, stray raindrops.

As they whisked inside, Mr. Buzz called out, "I shall join you in a moment, my dear. Our trunks are here, but I must find my small portmanteau."

A round, small, cheerful-looking man came bustling out of the hotel just as Darsie was wondering whether a portmanteau was the same as a satchel. Spying Mr. Buzz, the cheerful gentleman bowed excitedly three times and then, after a moment's hesitation, a fourth time for good measure.

"My dear, dear sir! Welcome to the Eagle Hotel. I am Henry Buehler, and I have the honor to be the proprietor. You distinguish us by your visit, indeed you do, sir!"

Mr. Buehler took a deep breath, beamed, and went on more calmly. "I have given orders that your party is to have the best chambers in the house, and I shall have your luggage sent up at once. We trust that you will be most comfortable with us. My wife has desired me to place her little parlor at your disposal so that you may dine and receive guests in privacy."

Mr. Buzz shook the hotelkeeper's hand vigorously. "That is kind of you, sir. Most kind!" He gave an anxious glance in the direction of the coach. "I shall follow you, sir, as soon as I can put my hand on my small case. It is black leather. A portmanteau."

"Mister?" Darsie gave a tug at the sleeve of Mr. Buzz's fur coat. "Is this here black bag a pootmanto?"

Mr. Buzz's eyebrows shot up in surprise, and then he smiled. "Why, so it is! Are you an hotel baggageman, young sir?"

"Heck, no!" Darsie exclaimed. "I'm Darsie Dobbs. I'm a horse driver for the *Betty D.*"

The gentleman's smile gave way to a faint, startled frown. "Who, or what, pray, may the *Betty D.* be?"

Small Darsie gave him a look of disgust. "Cap'n Dobbs's freight boat o' course. Best dang float on the whole Main Line Canal."

"Ah," Mr. Buzz said with an apologetic air. "I'm not a Pennsylvanian, you see, so I am not yet acquainted with the Main Line and its boats."

Darsie nodded. "I thought you was from somewheres else—from the queer way you talk."

The corners of Mr. Buzz's mouth twitched, but in a moment the earnest frown returned. "Do you *really* drive a towhorse? It seems a very tall job for such a small boy."

"Naw," Darsie said stoutly. "I ain't so small as all that."

"Nevertheless, I am sure it is hard work. I take it Captain Dobbs is your papa. Is he a kind master?"

For a moment Darsie seemed puzzled by the question, but

then he replied, "He don't beat me when I make mistakes, like other fellows' paps do. He just roars." He eyed Mr. Buzz with interest. "Have you got a little boy?"

"Indeed I have. Two of them, one very new, and one who is almost five. And two little girls. Have you any sisters, Master Dobbs?"

Darsie nodded. "Three of 'em. There's Cherry and Merry, and Ellen. Ellen's the baby. An' there's Sam—him and Cherry is twins—and Mam and Pap, and Dogberry. He's our dog."

Mr. Buzz laughed, then looked up as the coachman stuck his head in at the door of his vehicle to address the remaining passengers. "That's two for the White Hall Hotel an' three for the Red Lion, an' the rest for the canal basin. Right? Right."

At the words "canal basin," Darsie felt a guilty little stab of alarm. His eyes slid to Mr. Buzz's open coat and the gold chain draped across his waistcoat to his watch pocket.

"Hi, Mister?" He gave a tug at the gentleman's sleeve. "What o'clock is it?"

Mr. Buzz's eyebrows quirked up in amusement as he pulled out his watch to consult it. "Just gone half past six." Seeing Darsie's look of distress, he bent to ask kindly, "Are you late for your supper? I hope you won't be roared at."

"I ain't sure how to get straight back," Darsie confessed in a small voice. "An' if I ain't back afore pitch dark, Pap *might* whup me." It wasn't strictly a fib. He might, but of course he wouldn't.

Mr. Buzz patted Darsie's head. "Come, come. No need to worry, young Dobbs. Here is your rescuer at hand." He straightened and called up to the coach driver, who had mounted to his seat and taken up the reins.

"Coachman! Another passenger for the canal basin. Will a quarter dollar pay this young man's fare?"

"Shoo, ten cents'll do it," the driver said. He stretched down a hand. "Here, give'm a boost up."

The next thing Darsie knew, he was seated beside the coachman and his nephew on the driver's high perch, looking down on the broad backs of the four big horses. "Gee-yup!" the driver cried, and with a slap of the reins and a sharp snap of his whip, he swung the lumbering coach away from the hotel portico and up the puddle-shiny street.

Darsie twisted around to call out "Much obliged!" to Mr. Buzz, but he was too small to see past the driver's bulk and his flapping purple sleeves. Then, on a long, straight stretch of Walnut Street, the driver took him up on his knees and offered to let him hold and slap the reins. Darsie forgot Mr. Buzz entirely and, as the team of horses stepped out smartly, let out a long, high whoop of delight.

3

Thursday Evening

Two hours later and an hour north of Harrisburg, Cherry brought a fourth steaming mug of coffee up the short, steep stair from the *Betty D.*'s cubbyhole of a galley kitchen. She frowned at Captain Dobbs as if she were a disapproving parent and he a guilty small boy.

"It's a good thing I wasn't fetching you more coffee when you whanged us into the lock gate back yonder. It would have sloshed all over," she said sternly. "How *could* you, Pap? After all the bragging Sam and I do about how fine a hand on the tiller you are! Mr. Hatter looked like he was going to have an apoplexy fit."

"It wasn't such a hard bump," Captain Dobbs protested meekly in between sips of the strong, black coffee. "We didn't leave so much as a mark on the gate timbers."

"I don't know why not," Cherry grumbled, rather unfairly, since the bump, as bumps go, had been more of a nudge than a blow. She reached her hand out for the mug as the captain drained it. "I'll bring some more."

"*More?*" Captain Dobbs groaned. "I feel like I've got a gallon sloshing around belowdecks already. Have a heart, Cherry my gal! It's not like I was the worse for drink. One rum and molasses, that's all I had. One. Just to be sociable. Truly, nary a drop more. It was the fiddlin' took me to Tom Boak's. You know how I do love a fiddle-down. How was I to know the axle on that freight wagon'd get fixed so double-quick?"

Cherry shook her head. "Like Mam says, one glass of spirits is as good as a pint pot full when you haven't got a head for it. It wouldn't be so bad if you just got loud and cheery, Pap. But you get so fearful friendly. Mister Boak said you stood drinks twice for everybody all 'round. And," she accused, "you forgot all about the book money."

Captain Dobbs made an unhappy face. "Now *that* I'm really sorry for, my dear. If we had only seventy-five cents more to spare, you could have had your *Emmeline* and that Rollo book as well. Next time. I promise you."

"It's all right, Pap." Cherry gave him a quick peck of a kiss, taking care to keep clear of the tiller. "I can use Merry's school eraser to get the scribbles out of *Nicholas Nickleby,* and the lost pages are all at the front. That's better than the middle or the end."

"That's my gal! I reckon I could do with a bit of supper now. How about you slice me some bread and fry up some bacon to go with it."

Cherry vanished down the steps into the tiny galley. By the time she reappeared with six thick, hot bacon slices between two slabs of bread on a tin plate, the boat was slowing for the approach to Dauphin Lock.

The *Betty D.* slid into the lock as silkily as the night breeze that whispered along the water. It came to a stop a perfect foot from the upstream gates. Satisfied that her pap's head was clear at last, Cherry decided to steal an hour's rest once they were through the lock and underway again. Her father would never hear of her taking over the tiller after dark, and the next lock, Twin Taverns, was more than an hour ahead. She lifted the coffeepot from the stove to a trivet, and stepped through the narrow door in the back galley wall into the tiny family cabin. There she tugged off her boots and climbed wearily into the bunk above the one where Darsie lay.

She was fast asleep before she could draw her blanket up —fast asleep and dreaming of Darsie's Mr. Buzz presenting her with his dashing fur coat, and Mr. Goodge the bookseller eyeing the coat and whispering, "Just tap her on the noggin an' take it," while Pap sat on the bar at Boak's Tavern and fiddled away to the tune of "The Sailor's Hornpipe," and Dogberry danced with Sam.

Sam, out on the towpath, was far from dancing. Though the rain had lightened to a drizzle, ankle-deep mud clung to his boots. His feet looked and felt as heavy as an elephant's. Three hours of his six-hour shift still to go! He sighed and trudged on, thankful at least that so few downstream boats had passed. Darsie and Pap were the lucky ones! Darsie was too little to drive even a short shift at night, and because navigating the canal—and the Susquehanna River crossing —at night was tricky, Captain Dobbs's experienced hand had to stay on the tiller.

Much of the time the moon and stars were hidden by clouds. That made the stumping along on elephant feet no easier. The canal followed the Susquehanna River up its gorge, with the towpath running atop a bank between canal and river. The river showed as a darker blackness on the left. On the right hand only the glimmers on the water from the *Betty D.*'s prow and stern lanterns showed where the canal left off and the far bank began. When the clouds scudded away from the moon, the hills above the canal loomed high, and the broad river shimmered like Preacher Dinkelspiel's wife's blue-black Sunday silk dress.

Sam, as he slogged along behind Grinny, slapped the reins gently on the big gelding's rump and tried to think what it would be like to be full grown and captain of his own boat. Cherry might spin imaginary adventures peopled with dastardly villains and daring heroines; Sam's imagination, for all his love of book adventures, did not soar so high.

First off, to be a captain, he ought to get married as soon as he got a boat. Without a wife, and then kids, to be drivers and deckhands, a captain had to pay for hired hands. And hired hands cost too much. Perhaps he could marry Daisy Mossberger. Or Emma Dumpleman. The *Daisy D.* would be a prettier name for a boat than the *Emma D.*, but Emma herself was nearly as pretty as Daisy, and a lot cheerier. . . .

In the middle of this daydream, the drumming of hoofbeats banished Emma Dumpleman's curly red hair and turned-up nose from his thoughts. Sam found himself alone with Grinny on the dark towpath.

He swung around in alarm. Hoofbeats? A passenger packet's towing team? Surely not this late out of Harrisburg! Pap had given no call to slacken the towline. Nor did any riding lights glimmer down-canal from the *Betty D.* What—?

After a moment, Sam let out a "Whew!" of relief. The horses coming up so fast were not coming up the towpath side, but on the road along the right-hand side of the canal.

The clouds scudded away from the moon as the horses loped past and around the bend ahead, and Sam saw the horses and their riders—one tall and one dumpy—clearly against the moon-silvered road and trees.

The tall rider wore a high-crowned hat with a long, crooked feather that flapped as he rode.

4

Friday Morning, March 25th

"Mind what you're at! Hold still," Cherry warned as she tipped the last of the breakfast coffee into Sam's tin mug. "What's so all-fired interesting over in Hack Martin's meadow, anyhow?"

The *Betty D.*, with Sam at the tiller, was making a good two and a half miles an hour—even with a lock to navigate every mile and a half or so. During the night they had left the Susquehanna and headed west on the Juniata River portion of the canal, traveling as far as the Martin farm outside of Millerstown. The Dobbses knew many of the farmers along the Juniata River because they often bought milk and eggs and an occasional chicken for Sunday dinner from them. Most other canallers didn't bother to pay for chicken dinners that strayed too near the towpath.

Sam stared past Darsie and the plodding Grinny to the Martin meadow between the canal and the stream that ran along the foot of Wildcat Ridge. "Them horses!" he exclaimed. "It *is* them."

"*Those* horses," Cherry said sternly.

"Those horses, then. The piebald and the bay." He pointed. "I saw that piebald's spots last night. They're the same horses as passed us t'other side of Clark's Ferry. Them—those two smelly lookin' fellers were up on 'em. I swear to goodness it was them. They were goin' fast as rabbits with a hound on their tails."

Cherry, who had ducked back down into the tiny galley, forgot about measuring more coffee into the speckled enamel coffeepot. "*What* smelly fellows?" She bounded up the short stair. "*Where?*"

"Never you mind." Captain Dobbs came through from the cabin, where he had been snatching a nap, and followed her up. "Millerstown Lock's comin' along before you know it. I'll take the tiller. Sam, you hop out there and take over the drivin'. Tell Darsie he c'n ride Grinny into Millerstown if he's a mind to, 'stead of comin' aboard at the bridge up ahead."

Lifting the *Betty D.*'s battered trumpet to his lips, he blew a brisk *too-too-too-it!*

"*What* fellows?" Cherry almost shrieked as Sam dashed up the steps to the cabin roof and snatched up the vaulting pole.

"Mebbe you didn't notice 'em," Sam said. As his leap landed him on the towpath, he called back, "They were comin' out of old man Goodge's back room. A podgy little man in a greasy brown coat? And a big lummox in a tall hat with—"

"—with a broken turkey feather stuck in the band!" Cherry finished breathlessly, remembering in a rush. In last night's hurry and bustle—rescuing their father from Boak's Tavern, seeing to the loading of the cargo of stoves, racing back to the book shop for *Nicholas Nickleby,* and worrying over Darsie's tardy return—she had entirely forgotten about the conversation she had overheard through Mr. Goodge's office wall.

"Why didn't you tell me?" she yelled. In her excitement she danced a little jig. "Why didn't you tell me right away?"

"Lo-o-ock re-ead-y?" Captain Dobbs bawled up-canal through his cupped hands.

"You was asleep," Sam called over his shoulder. He took the reins from Darsie and boosted his little brother up onto Grinny's broad back. "Anyhow, why should I?"

"Re-ea-dee-ee!" came the halloo from up ahead. The first houses of Millerstown were already sliding past.

"Because they're thieves!" Cherry screeched. "Maybe even murderers. They were in Mr. Goodge's office. They were planning a dastardly plot. I heard them through the wall."

Captain Dobbs gave a loud guffaw. "Bless me, Cherry gal! You'd still be spinning stories if there was an earthquake in the middle of a tornado in the midst of a flood."

Cherry stamped her foot. "It's not a story, Pap. It's not!"

"Sla-a-ack!" Captain Dobbs boomed to Sam. "And you, missy," he said, "just you simmer down and get for'ard to haul that towrope aboard. Time enough when it's coiled all right and tight fer you t' tell me what in tarnation it is you're blithering about."

Cherry jumped to her job. The *Betty D.* had begun to slow. On the towpath, Sam loped ahead to lend a hand with opening the lock gate. Darsie and Grinny followed at a tired amble.

Once the towrope was aboard—in a coil no one, least of all Captain Dobbs, would call right or tight—Cherry raced back to her father at the tiller. In her impatience to get the story out she hopped up and down, but to her father's surprise she told it without any Cherry-style fancy touches. Captain Dobbs, before he turned his eye to keeping the *Betty D.* dead center as she coasted between the high lock gates, cast her a doubtful look.

"We ought to tell the town constable so he can arrest them, oughtn't we, Pap? *Oughtn't* we?" Cherry urged as she threw the aft mooring line up for Sam to snub around the stone bollard at lockside.

Captain Dobbs rubbed his stubbly chin as Cherry darted forward to throw up the forward mooring line.

"Well, now, Sis," he said, "what d'you have in mind to tell him? That just maybe he's got two fellers, one shortish an' one tallish, who're on foot, but just might be hoss thieves, and just maybe have it in mind to steal somethin' or other, but you don't know rightly what, or whether the somethin' or other happens to be here in Millerstown or somewheres else?"

"That's not fair, Pap! I can describe them two right down to their buttons and boots, and we know where the horses are." Cherry brightened. "Besides—"

"*Those* two, my gal." Captain Dobbs gave a sorrowful shake of his head. The little twitch of his mustache was suspiciously close to a smile. Cherry was so self-righteously schoolmarmish about Sam and Darsie's "ain'ts" and "not no-hows" that it may have tickled him to find a chance to chide her for bad grammar. It wasn't often that anyone spotted a chance to—except, of course, for Mrs. Dobbs. Mrs. Dobbs was as fair-spoken as any parson's wife or banker's lady, but then she had an Aunt Bessie who was a schoolmarm. As a girl she had dreamed of being one herself. Young Cherry, though, had set about polishing up her own nouns and pro-nouns and auxiliary verbs only when she got the bee in her bonnet about becoming a story writer.

Cherry's mind was not on grammar. "Those," she amended absently. "And it's not so. I *do* know something about the something or other. I just remembered. It's got a front, and the front has something written on it. Mr. Goodge told those men so. He said, 'It'll likely have something like this written on the front'—or something like that."

"Something like something-something-something?" Cap-tain Dobbs nodded solemnly. "I reckon it's purty serious af-ter all."

"Pap!" Cherry wailed in protest.

Sam's hoot of laughter rang out from above, where he leaned out over the lock's stone wall to watch the *Betty D.* ride up on the rising water.

Cherry looked up. "It isn't funny, knothead," she snapped angrily.

"'Tis too, featherbrain."

Captain Dobbs broke in sharply. "That'll be enough of

that. Truth to tell, I reckon it might not be a bad idea all in all to tip a neighborly hint to the constable. I figure if two fellers ride up to town and leave behind a couple of hosses as could be stolen, then plot or no, they just might steal them a fresh pair to head on west with."

"I'll go," Sam said. He scrambled to his feet from where he had been kneeling at lockside to look down on the *Betty D.* The boat had slowed its rise as the water level in the lock neared that of the upstream canal.

"Not without me," Cherry objected quickly. "Don't you dare. Pap, tell him so!"

Leaping lockside from a boat rail was against all the rules or she would have leaped to follow Sam. It was too dangerous, though. If you slipped down between the boat and the lock wall, you might as well be a smear of butter.

Captain Dobbs's eye was caught by a sign from the lockkeeper. He held up a hand.

"Hold your britches, the both of you. Sam, you step smart and loose them ropes, then give Mr. Beeman a hand with the lock gate. Cherry, you stow the ropes an' stand by with the towline. We'll go on an' tie up past the town wharf if it's clear. Time enough then for the two of you t' chase up the constable. Go on, hop to it!"

They hopped.

While the *Betty D.* was still riding at low water in the lock chamber, none of the Dobbses had seen the short, fat man in a newish but too tight green coat and shiny boots who approached the lockkeeper's house, tipped his hat to Mrs. Beeman, and asked a polite question.

Mrs. Beeman was used to men who shaved only on Saturday nights, so thought nothing of the man's stubble of beard. She did wonder afterward, though, that a gentleman with a fresh, clean shirt and face should have such a very dirty neck and fingernails.

5

Friday Evening and Early Saturday Morning, March 26th

"So Pap give us ten minutes," Sam told his mother when the whole family had gathered in the keeping room of the Dobbses' little house that evening. "And Mr.—"

" 'Pap *give* us'?" Mrs. Dobbs tucked her chin down and prissed her lips up in what the children called her "Aunt Bessie" face. "Tut-tut, I do declare!"

Seven-year-old Merry giggled as she turned the sausages that sizzled in the big iron skillet on the fireplace trivet. The wide fireplace took up half of one wall of the snug keeping room that took up all of the ground floor of the little house and served both as kitchen and parlor. Merry, like Sam and Cherry before her, was staying at home and going to school until she could read. Next year she would go back to work on the canal and it would be Darsie's turn at school.

Sam grinned. Unlike Cherry, his mam didn't much mind his sounding like a canaller aboard the *Betty D.*, but she drew a firm line straight across the foot of the wharf at the

Dobbses' tiny canalside farm. Once at home again, Sam had to watch his grammar.

"Gave," he amended. "Anyhow, Mr. Beeman told us where to find the town lockup, and when we got there, Cherry told the constable about her patchy old plot."

"All moonshine and cobwebs, I still say," Captain Dobbs observed through a puff of pipe smoke. He sat in the rocker beside the fireplace and dandled Baby Ellen happily on his knee. Old Dogberry, the barrel-stout terrier, watched accusingly, as if he expected his master at any moment to drop the baby on her head.

"That's what the constable thought, too," said an indignant Cherry. " 'Flimsy flapdoodle,' he called it."

"But he did say he'd ride over to the Martin farm to ask about the horses," Sam said.

"Hmph!" Cherry sniffed. "When? A week from next Tuesday?"

Mrs. Dobbs lifted a pot lid to test a boiling potato for doneness. "Bless me, with stolen horses and a dastardly plot and Darsie's Mr. Buzz, you've had a lively time of it so far this trip!"

"This crew brew up their own lively times," said Captain Dobbs. "They stir in a teaspoon of fact, a will-o'-the-wisp or two, a cup of invention, a pint of wishing and a quart of canal water. Today's brew tastes more like a storybook concoction than ever."

"Storybooks!" Mrs. Dobbs looked up from patting Wednesday's leftover potato into two flat cakes for a treat for Captain Dobbs. The rest of the family would have to settle for fresh-boiled-and-buttered. "I declare, I quite forgot! What about Cherry's errand in Harrisburg? Are we to have the beginning of a new book after supper?"

"Yes, the book!" Young Merry looked up eagerly from making room among the sputtering sausages for the potato cakes to come. "Did you get a Rollo book?"

Cherry clapped her hands. She had scarcely thought of the new book since her return to Goodge's Book Shop to buy it.

"*Nicholas Nickleby!* It's still down on the *Betty D.*" She pulled her coat from its peg on the back of the door.

"Not now, Cherry," her mother cautioned. "We'll be dishing up supper in a few moments."

Her warning was wasted. Cherry had already snatched up a lantern and was out the door into the dusk and racing down the footpath between the pasture and the chicken run.

"You don't want a Rollo book," Sam told Merry as the door slammed. "Mrs. Huffnagle read us *Rollo's Vacation* in third grade. It was all right, I s'pose, but Rollo and his friends were so goody-goody and all-fired polite that I pretty near wore out my jaw from yawning."

Captain Dobbs chortled. "You sound like your twin sis," he said.

Mrs. Dobbs smiled. "Well, his twin sis has worked her usual magic and vanished just when I need an extra pair of hands. Sam, you'll have to set out the plates and cups and cutlery while I fetch the applesauce and what's left of yesterday's rabbit pie."

41

By the time Cherry returned with her neat brown-paper parcel, Baby Ellen was drowsing in her cradle and supper was on the table. After three days of bread and Cherry's under-fried bacon and over-fried eggs, the sausages, potatoes, applesauce, and leftovers were as good as a feast to the crew of the *Betty D.* The best of all came last: sugared apples baked in the fireplace dutch oven.

By the time the potato pot was scoured, the table scrubbed, and the last fork returned to the cutlery box, Baby Ellen was fast asleep and Darsie was curled up beside Dogberry on the hearthrug. Cherry unwrapped *Nicholas Nickleby,* put the paper aside to smooth out later and save, and handed the book to her mother.

"Ah, it's by Mr. Dickens!" Mrs. Dobbs said, with a note of pleased surprise. "And here I thought you children didn't much care for the other Dickens book we read."

"The Pickwick Papers." Captain Dobbs's eyebrows shot up. "'Course they liked it. A tip-top tale!"

Cherry thought that Mr. Pickwick and his friends were a pack of old sillies, but said only, "This one is different. I read some bits in it."

Mrs. Dobbs frowned as she opened the cover. "But, Cherry . . ."

There was no title page. After the frontispiece came a gap along the book's spine where the opening chapters had fallen out after long, hard use. The first page, numbered 41, was headed chapter 3, with a brief "title" in tiny lettering that read:

Mr. Ralph Nickleby receives Sad Tidings of his Brother, but bears up nobly against the Intelligence communicated to him. The Reader is informed how he liked Nicholas, who is herein introduced, and how kindly he proposed to make his Fortune at once.

"There, you see," said Cherry. She pointed eagerly. "The book is about Nicholas, and it says he wasn't in the first two chapters, so we won't miss so very much. Besides, the book cost only twenty-five cents."

"We didn't have much cash after Pap paid the collector." Sam spoke quickly, with a frown at his sister.

"Even less after their pap paid for drinks all around at the fiddle-down at Boak's Tavern," Captain Dobbs confessed sheepishly. "I feel real bad about that. Honest Injun, Sis: Next trip you'll have the other seventy-five cents. You can buy that *Emmeline* book you wanted."

Mrs. Dobbs put on her Aunt Bessie face. "I reckon," she said, "that it's just as well April's almost here and summer's just around the corner. As soon as school's out for Merry, she and Ellen and I'll be back aboard the *Betty D.* to keep an eye on you four!"

"Can't be a bit too soon for me," the Captain agreed with a twinkle as he took Darsie up on his lap. "Now, let's have us some of this *Nicholas Niggly*."

Cherry giggled. "*Nicholas Nickleby,* Pap!"

"Right. You start us off, Cherry gal."

Everyone but Darsie and Baby Ellen took a turn at the reading. Merry had to go slowly, sounding out the words she did not know yet. Darsie dozed, but stirred and sat up as the nasty schoolmaster, Mr. Squeers, beat the little boy who sneezed. Afterward, everyone (except Darsie, who had fallen asleep again) agreed that it would be hard to wait until the *Betty D.*'s return from Hollidaysburg for the next installment. Mr. Squeers, they said, was a dreadful, wicked man, but the stony-hearted Mr. Ralph Nickleby gave them the shivers, too. Nicholas would do well to mistrust his uncle. Oddest of all was Newman Noggs, old Nickleby's assistant. Sam particularly admired Mr. Noggs's prodigious knuckle-cracking.

Darsie, half waking on being carried up to his cot in the loft at the finish of chapter 4, had announced sleepily, "If Mrs. Huffnagle at Merry's school beats little boys when they sneeze, I'm not *never* going there."

Once everyone was snug in bed, Sam began to practice cracking his own knuckles quietly under his quilt.

Mrs. Dobbs was up and out collecting eggs—and chickens—at the first touch of dawn. Captain Dobbs had already harnessed the horses and led them from the barn down to the wharf alongside the canal. By the time Mrs. Dobbs returned to the little farmhouse the coffeepot was boiling on its fireplace trivet. A sleepy-eyed Cherry was slicing strips from the last side of bacon from last year's pigs.

"Is Darsie stirring yet?" asked Mrs. Dobbs.

"He's got as far as the stretching and groaning part." Cherry yawned.

"Here—these are for breakfast." Her mother took enough

eggs from her basket to fill the shallow wooden bowl on the table. "I'm toting the rest down to the canal. The express packet ought to be coming along soon."

"Um, yuh-uhm," said Cherry.

Mrs. Dobbs exchanged her faded farm bonnet for her second best, and pinned her going-to-market shawl on over her coat.

"Dogberry!" she called.

The stout little terrier, one ear down and one stiffly up even when he slept, twitched, sat up in his bed beside the chimney, and yawned. At the sight of the bonnet, shawl, and egg basket he stumbled out of bed, staggered stiffly across to the door, and then, taking a pause to stretch, barked long and loud, as if to say, "Everybody up! Everybody out! Stir a leg! Sharp, now! Sharp, now!"

"Hush your yapping, you rowdy little ruckus," Cherry yelped. She snatched up a heel of bread to throw at him.

Dogberry caught the bread neatly and whisked out through the door ahead of his mistress to lead the way down the narrow track to the canal. Mrs. Dobbs took up a heavy second basket from the doorstep, and followed. She went slowly, taking care in the half light not to put a foot wrong on the rutted path.

The *Betty D.* was moored at the foot of the path. Grinny and Bell stood dozing on the wharf beside her, their reins looped around a snubbing post. As she passed the boat on her way to the humpbacked bridge some yards upstream, Mrs. Dobbs took up a stick to knock beside the cabin window.

"Up, Sam! There's breakfast to eat and a horse to bring aboard!"

When the *Betty D.* was carrying a cargo it was not safe to leave her unmanned, even when the cargo was made up of items as lumpish as iron stoves. Indeed, there were tales aplenty of thieves taking off with cargo, boat, and all if the horses or mules were left in their stables aboard. That was why when spending a night at home, Captain Dobbs always took Bell and Grinny off to the barn, and Sam slept on board with the cargo. Sam had a loud bell to ring out the cabin window if he heard unexpected footsteps on deck in the night.

By the time Sam was on his way back up to the house, leaving Dogberry in charge of the horses, Mrs. Dobbs had deposited her baskets on the bridge and dragged up a back-less chair she kept under a nearby bush for packet-watching. With sometimes forty and more hungry passengers to feed, cooks on the better-class packets counted on buying fresh eggs and milk and other produce along the way. The five hens under the tied-down lid of the second basket would very likely be a tasty stew by suppertime.

Mrs. Dobbs shivered in the morning cold. Even so, she was about to doze off when she heard a faint wisp of a call from down-canal. "Low bridge!" A moment later she spied a far-off figure approaching along the towpath. The packet was not far behind. Soon she could make out the first figure to be a gentleman bundled up in hat and muffler and greatcoat, striding briskly along some distance ahead of the packet's towhorses.

As the gentleman came abreast of the *Betty D.* he gave the boat a sharp look. Spying Mrs. Dobbs on the bridge ahead, he raised his hat and called out, "Good morning to you, madam."

"Good morning, sir," said Mrs. Dobbs.

Dogberry, mistrustful of strangers on foot, gave a growl and barreled along to the narrow bridge and over it and down onto the towpath. Planting himself in its middle, he dared the stranger to pass.

"Grr-rr-rowf!"

The gentleman stopped, then laughed aloud. "Upon my honor, this must be Dogberry! And you, madam, will be Mrs. Dobbs." He bowed.

"Why, yes, but—" Mrs. Dobbs was surprised and flustered.

"My apologies, madam. I did not mean to startle you." He smiled. "I saw the name *Betty D.* on the boat, and concluded the rest. I heard something of Dogberry and your family from Master Darsie Dobbs in Harrisburg."

"Ah," said Mrs. Dobbs. "Would you be Darsie's Mr. Buzz?"

He laughed again. "I would indeed, madam!"

The packet boat, towed by four horses in tandem, was coming up fast, and at the cry of "Low bridge!" Mr. Buzz tipped his hat again. "Good day, madam. I must keep ahead of the horses or I shall be left behind before the next lock. My regards to Master Darsie."

No sooner had Mr. Buzz disappeared along the towpath under the bridge than a hail rang out from the cook on the packet, and the driver slowed his horses. Several gentleman passengers sitting on the roof crouched low in order not to have their heads cracked against the bridge. They watched their cook's hustle-bustle with interest. In amazingly short order he had leaped ashore, large sack and empty egg basket in hand, and darted along to the bridge. There, after a moment's haggling over the price, he popped the five hens from the basket into his sack, secured it with a string, and dropped it onto the cabin roof as the boat nosed under the bridge. Trading the empty egg basket for the full one, he crossed to the upstream side of the bridge. From there, as the packet picked up speed again, he dropped nimbly back onto the roof-deck.

Mrs. Dobbs was in just as great a hurry. Thrusting the egg and chicken money into her coat pocket, she snatched up the two baskets in one hand and her long skirt in the other, and ran. She ran down the bridge, past the *Betty D.*, up the meadow path, and in through the farmhouse door as fast as any tomboy schoolgirl. An excited Dogberry dashed around her in agitated circles, barking wildly all the way. Twice he almost tripped his mistress before he charged back down the path to check on the horses.

Mrs. Dobbs burst in through the farmhouse door. Captain Dobbs looked up from his breakfast, then leaped to his feet as she flung the baskets to the floor and dashed to the fireplace.

"Betty, gal! What the divil's happened? What's afoot?"

Mrs. Dobbs made no answer. She snatched *Nicholas Nick-*

leby from the mantel shelf, plumped herself down in the fire-side rocker, and opened the book to the frontispiece.

"Oh, mercy, mercy me!" She looked up from the portrait printed there, her eyes round in wonder. "Oh, *Darsie!*"

"Mam, what is it?" cried Sam and Cherry and Merry all together.

"Darsie's Mr. Buzz—" she said breathlessly. "He's not 'Buzz.' He's *'Boz'!*" She held out the open book.

Beneath the engraved portrait of a handsome, dark-haired, youngish man, they read

The Celebrated "Boz"
Mr. Charles Dickens

6

For a moment the Dobbses' keeping room was quiet enough to hear an ant walk across the floor. Then Captain Dobbs, Merry, Sam, and Cherry spoke all at once.

"I'll be blowed!" said the Captain.

"He *can't* be him! Mr. Dickens lives in London, clear over in England," said Merry.

"Honest Injun, Mam? Golly, I wish I'd seen 'im. He could've wrote in our book," said Sam.

"It's a hoax, you sillies; Mam's just funning. Aren't you, Mam?"

"I am *not* funning, Charity Ann Dobbs." Mrs. Dobbs was indignant. "If I were one for swearing, why—I'd swear on the good book it was Mr. Dickens. Mr. 'Boz.' That was the pen name he used when he first became a writer, and that is why the newspapers called him 'the celebrated Boz' once he was famous. There is no famous 'Mr. Buzz.' "

"But—"

"Hang on!" Captain Dobbs dashed off excitedly toward the front door, where the coats hung on pegs. "Hang on to your britches," he said as he fished in his coat pocket.

In a moment he returned with a copy of the *Harrisburg Gazette*.

"I ain't—I haven't had a chance t' read more'n the front-page headings yet, but it seems t' me there was a piece down here somewheres. . . . Ha! Here it is!"

Holding the paper out at arm's length, Captain Dobbs read aloud from an item in the bottom corner:

CELEBRATED AUTHOR TO TOUR KEYSTONE STATE

Admirers of Mr. Charles Dickens, the celebrated Author of *Pickwick Papers* and other popular works, will be interested to learn that our Correspondent in Baltimore informs us that "Boz" and his party plan to leave behind the Balls and Levees and crowded Receptions they have graced in New York, Washington, and Richmond, to travel across our fair State of Pennsylvania by coach and canal boat. We venture to predict that Mr. Dickens will view no grander or more stirring prospects on his journey westward to St. Louis than those afforded by the majestic gorge of the Susquehanna River and that Eighth Wonder of the World, the Por-

51

tage Railway over the summit of the magnificent Allegheny Mountains. We have it on good authority that Mr. Dickens intends to publish an Account of his American Travels, and we look forward to a Description of our own unmatched Landscape from his eloquent Pen.

Cherry snatched the paper from her father as he finished and read the item through again.

Mrs. Dobbs's dark eyes shone. "By canal boat! You see!" Her cheeks were as rosy as apples. "It *was* Mr. Dickens I spoke with."

"And me!" Darsie chimed in excitedly. "I talked to him *lots*. I guess I pretty near talked his hind leg off."

"I wish I'd seen him," Merry said longingly. "So's I could tell everybody at school. Oh, Pap, couldn't we follow after the packet in the *Betty D.*? Then if they stop in Lewistown . . ."

Sam snorted. "That's daft. The Pioneer Express packet is pretty near as fast as the new *General Armstrong* is cracked up to be, and we're loaded up with iron stoves. We'd never catch 'em up."

"Depends." Captain Dobbs rubbed his unshaven chin and squinted his eyes half shut. "Depends how long—"

Cherry gasped and clasped the newspaper to her chest. "Oh! *Oh!* Oh, Pap, we *must* follow the Express." Her eyes were almost as round and shiny as Sam's prized agate marbles.

She looked from her parents' blank stares to Merry's hopeful and Sam's startled ones.

"You needn't stare at me like an owl in a thundershower, Sam Dobbs," she said. "Don't you see? Those two men—Mr. Goodge's thieves—it's Mr. Dickens's travel book they're after. So Mr. Goodge can print it up and make pots and pots of money."

Cherry caught at her father's hand to tug him toward the front door. "Everybody fetch your coats!"

"Now, just a danged minute," Captain Dobbs began. "Goodge couldn't—"

"Hush!" Mrs. Dobbs raised both hands to stop the babble of voices that sprang up. "Hush! Cherry may be right. If she is, we have no time to argue, no time to waste. We must just *go*. Explanations later."

Everyone flew to snatch coats from the pegs by the front door. Merry scooped up two loaves of bread and the dish of eggs. Mrs. Dobbs snatched up Baby Ellen from her baby basket. Cherry followed with the basket itself. In no time flat, the Dobbs family, coats flapping and hats crammed on every which way from backward to sideways, had streamed out the front door of the little log and plank house and down the long, narrow path to the canal. Sam brought up the rear with the last of his ham and eggs folded up in a thick slice of bread.

Dogberry, stationed on the wharf beside Bell and big, sleepy, dapple-gray Grinny, dropped the big gelding's reins when he saw Captain Dobbs's long, lean legs come pumping down the path with all the rest behind, and set to barking wildly. *"Yap-yap-yap-yap-YAP!"* he cried, bouncing excitedly up and down. He dashed up the towpath at a furious pace, then wheeled to scramble back. *"Yap-yap-YAP-yap-yap-yap-YAP!"*

"Git outa my way, you hairy overstuffed sausage!" Captain Dobbs roared as he swerved clear of Dogberry's rush.

Grinny and Bell nickered and backed up nervously, tossing their heads so that the harness bells jingled, and showing the whites of their eyes.

"Hitch 'em both up, Sam," his father ordered.

"Whoa 'ere! 'Sall ri'!"

Sam caught at Grinny's headstall, gave Bell a clap on the shoulder, and made soothing ham-and-egg-sandwich-muffled noises until he could swallow the last bulging mouthful of his breakfast. Then hitching Grinny's harness to Bell's, he urged them along to the bridge and up over it and down to the towpath. When Cherry threw the end of the towrope out from the *Betty D.* he was ready with the ring chained to the spreader stick at the back end of Bell's harness. He tied the rope fast with a double rolling hitch, took up the reins, and cried, "Gee-*YUP!*"

Grinny and Bell set off so smartly that Sam almost lost his balance and tumbled into the raspberry brambles at the side of the towpath.

The family was already settled aboard. Merry was coiling up the mooring ropes, Cherry pushing with a barge pole to nudge the *Betty D.* clear of the wharf, Darsie filling the woodbox beside the galley stove from the restocked woodpile on deck, Captain Dobbs manning the tiller, and Mrs. Dobbs settling Baby Ellen in her basket on the family cabin floor. Merry finished first and hurried forward to hang over the rail at the bow of the boat, where she peered eagerly upstream. Her hope that the Express might still be in sight was dashed, but the faster boat *might* be stopped just around the next bend, her towrope snagged on a tree root, perhaps, or a hole stove in her prow by a submerged log.

"We're so *poky*," Merry wailed. Grinny and Bell leaned into their harness but the *Betty D.* slid away from the bank as slowly as if the canal were full of molasses.

"It's those dratted iron stoves," Cherry grumbled as she joined her sister at the rail.

"Don't get yourselves in a pucker, gals," Captain Dobbs called from his post at the tiller. "The Express is likely already slowing down for Lewistown. We've got about as much chance of catchin' 'em up as a tortoise after a hop-rabbit."

Darsie came back to sit on the bench that ran along the *Betty D.*'s stern, behind the tiller.

"But the tortoise *beat* the hare in the story," he said. "Ain't that right, Pap?"

Mrs. Dobbs, coming up through the galley from the family cabin, heard and laughed.

"He has you there, Daniel."

"Hmph! Never you mind. What I want to know, Betty m' dear, is just why we're skittering off after a fast packet a'*tall*. You know durned well old Goodge isn't sneaking 'round, snatching bits of books. He may be a penny-grubbing rascal,

55

but he can't go printing up and selling stolen goods. He'd land himself in the Dauphin County lockup."

Mrs. Dobbs straightened her bonnet, then plumped herself down on the bench beside Darsie and set to tying the bonnet's strings.

"That's just it—he *wouldn't* land in the lockup. I believe Cherry has the right of it," she said.

"I told you so!" Cherry crowed. She rubbed her grimy hands on her apron as she came back across the rooftop deck with Merry trailing after her.

"I read a piece in the *Ladies' Quarterly* that explained it," Mrs. Dobbs said. "It seems our Congress has never passed a law like other countries have, which says that writers own what they write. That means printers and booksellers in our country can claim that what writers write are 'ideas,' not 'things,' and that ideas are free for anybody to take and use. And they *do* take them."

"Just like pirates?" Darsie was suddenly more interested. There were pirates on the canal, though he had never seen one.

"Exactly. Book pirates." His mother nodded. "Some even have 'spies' across the ocean, in England, who send the chapters of the new stories here by the very next ship when each new installment comes out in a magazine."

"But if those men snatch paper Mr. Dickens writes on, it *has* to be stealing," Merry said anxiously. "Hasn't it?"

"It does," Mrs. Dobbs agreed. "But the law says that they are only stealing the paper, not the words on it."

"Sounds a load of claptrap to me," rumbled an indignant Captain Dobbs. "It ain't right."

56

"But we can try to stop them anyhow, Pap, can't we?" Cherry hopped from foot to foot in her distress.

Captain Dobbs took a deep breath. "I reckon so. I reckon if our Cherry is right about these two yahoos, we'll just have to see if we can't put a spoke in old Goodge's wheel."

"Oh, Pap!" Cherry flung her arms around her father with a loud *whoop*.

"Easy! Easy there!" Captain Dobbs corrected the tiller as the *Betty D.* made a short zig toward the center of the channel. "I don't see as there's much we can do if we miss the Express at Lewistown, but dang it, we'll have us a try."

As the Juniata River, the canal, and the *Betty D.* came up out of the deep Lewistown Narrows and around the foot of Shade Mountain, Bell and Grinny were stepping out at a brisk three and a half miles an hour, heavy cargo or no.

The Dobbses passed three floats—two freights and a raft of fresh-cut logs—headed down-canal. Each reported passing the Express "a fair piece back."

From their perch on the boat's prow, Cherry and Merry could see snatches of the widening river valley between the clumps of willow trees along the curve ahead. Now and again, they could see the wharf warehouses beyond the Lewistown lock, over a mile away. Cherry squinted.

"I don't see 'em, Pap," Merry shrilled.

"They must be inside the lock," Cherry called over her shoulder.

Sam gave the horses a slap of the reins. "Stable, Grinny! Stable, Bell!"

At the magic word Grinny and Bell leaned into their harness harder yet. No longer young, and too often bone-tired, they could still be as strong-hearted as Gringolet and Bellerophon, the famous long-ago horses whose names they bore.

Even at an amazing four miles an hour, the tree-rimmed bank seemed only to inch by. The pause between Captain Dobbs's *Too-too-too-it!* on the horn and his bellow of *"Lo-o-o-ock ready?"* felt more like half an hour than five minutes. By the time the Lewistown lockkeeper's *"Re-e-ea-dee!"* came floating back, Cherry was wild with frustration.

"I could *swim* faster'n this," she groaned.

Merry drummed her heels against the *Betty D.*'s planking. *"Dogberry* could swim faster."

Dogberry, standing between them with his paws up on the gunnel rail, barked in agreement.

When at last the *Betty D.* coasted into place behind another freight boat waiting its turn in the lock, there was no Express in sight. A downstream packet was in the lock chamber, the packet berth at the town wharf was empty, and not a boat was to be seen in the stretch before the next bridge upstream.

"The Express?" The lockkeeper shouted his answer to Captain Dobbs's bellowed question. "She came through near twenty minutes ago. This ain't a reg'lar stop, so with no passengers to unload or take on, she didn't tie up."

The disappointed Dobbses gathered by the rail on the town wharf side. "What now, Pap?" Sam called across from the towpath.

Captain Dobbs lifted his hat and scratched his head.

Mrs. Dobbs drew a deep breath. "Well, the *Betty D.* has to go on, willy-nilly. Those iron stoves have to get to Hollidaysburg. I reckon I'll have to catch myself and Merry and Baby Ellen a ride back home on the next downstream float."

"Oh, Mam!" Merry wailed. "Mayn't I go with Sam and Cherry this trip?"

"And miss school on Monday? Certainly not!"

"Pap? *Please!*"

"No quibbles, now," Captain Dobbs said mildly. He settled his hat on firmly. "We'll tie up over here at the wharf. I'll trot along to the Town Hall and warn the law in case they clap an eye on those fellers. And you all can stay put and keep watch in case another packet or a fast freight comes along. If they was to catch up to the Express and the damage wasn't already done, they could tip Mr. Dickens to keep an eye peeled for mischief."

The children wore glum looks. But what else was there to be done?

Cherry could not bear to "stay put." With Sam in tow, she set off along the wharf toward the footbridge over the towpath for a better view back down the canal. Twenty minutes later, a horn sounded and a two-horse team came cantering into sight around the farthest bend. The short, stubby boat that skimmed along behind them rode the top of the wave her own prow ploughed up out of the water.

A puzzled Sam leaned out over the parapet of the bridge, the better to see. "Shoot! Ain't that the *Gospel Ark?* Parson

Golly must reckon he's got Old Nick and all his devils at his heels to be puttin' his horses in such a sweat. Why, they must be doin' six or seven miles an hour!"

Cherry did not take time to correct the "ain't"—or to frown at Sam's disrespectful nickname for the canalboat preacher. Cupping her hands, she shouted back toward the *Betty D., "Mam! The Ark! The Ark's coming!"* She waved wildly, pointing past the lock and the town. *"Tell Parson Golightly about Mr. Dickens!"*

From the bridge it was impossible to tell whether the parson got the message. Mrs. Dobbs had understood the waving and pointing, if not the shouts, but no sooner had the *Gospel Ark* been raised up by the water of the lock and the lock's gates been opened, than the parson's horses lunged forward once again. Mrs. Dobbs picked up her skirts and leaped ashore from the *Betty D.* She ran along the town wharf, shouting, but by the time she reached the end of the wharf, the *Ark* was already past and heading toward the bridge.

Cherry watched the preacher's little boat as it drew rapidly closer. "Six or seven miles an hour . . ." She considered. "Can she really go that fast?"

"A little float like that, with a good team and no load aboard?" Sam nodded. "Easy."

Cherry cupped her hands to shout at the approaching boat. "Hi, the *Ark!* Why so fast, Rev'rend?"

Parson Golightly tipped his broad-brimmed hat with the hand that wasn't on the tiller and bellowed back in his best Sunday-meeting boom.

60

"Mornin', Charity Ann. I have a joyful occasion on the canal this side of Mount Union this morning. A wedding. Alas, I got a late start."

Sam's head swiveled. "Cherry! What—"

Cherry had hitched up her apron and skirt, and climbed over the wooden rail. She stood on a narrow strip of bridge beam, holding on with one hand.

"What are you waiting for?" she asked Sam. "Hurry up, slow boat! We can catch us a ride back after we warn Mr. Dickens!"

She turned to face the oncoming *Ark* and jumped.

7

Cherry was in midair before Sam could shoot out an arm to stop her. He followed, but jumped almost too late, for he landed at the very rear of the *Ark*'s cabin roof.

Parson Jeremiah Golightly let go the tiller to throw up his hands in alarm. Recovering quickly, he called to the driver, his nine-year-old grandson, who was mounted on the lead horse. "All is well, Jem! Keep up the pace. Only eight miles more!"

Turning to the twins, the parson tried his best to scowl and speak sharply. "That, young man, is an excellent method of breaking an assortment of bones. What do you mean by it? First your estimable mother makes a hoydenish spectacle of herself on the Lewistown wharf, calling some nonsense about warning the Express packet that there may be bees aboard. And now this harum-scarum invasion! Pray explain yourselves."

Sam smothered a grin, and Cherry bit her cheeks to keep from smiling.

"Not bees, Parson. *Thieves,*" Cherry explained. "They're after Mr. Charles Dickens's travel book."

"It all sounds a trifle farfetched to me," Parson Golightly said with lifted eyebrows when he had heard Cherry and Sam's tale. "But not inherently unfeasible—not totally impossible, I calculate. Mr. Charles Dickens, you say! I have seen in the newspaper accounts from New York and points south that he has drawn great crowds of admirers at every turn. An unprincipled bibliopole—a dishonest bookseller, that is to say—might well attempt to, um, *borrow* a manuscript so as to copy it; might even counterfeit its retrieval."

Cherry looked blank.

"What's that?" Sam asked.

"He might return it to the author, pretending to have found it, or to have bought it from the thief."

"So that he could print it and sell copies, and still be safe!" Cherry gave Parson Golightly an admiring look. "I hadn't thought of that."

"Alas, the world is full of just such wickedness." The parson sighed. Then he brightened. "But if, as you say, the Express packet left the Lewistown lock little more than half an hour ago, we have an excellent chance of overtaking it before the next lock. Indeed, we *shall* do it. Confusion to the wicked, I say!"

*   *   *

63

While the parson steered a daring mid-canal course, ready to sweep past any slower boat as it lowered its towrope or to slacken his own and veer out of the way of oncoming traffic, Cherry and Sam set about making themselves useful. There were ropes to pay out and snub and coil at each lock, horses to walk and rub down while the *Gospel Ark* rode up on the rising water in the lock chamber, and lockkeepers to help in opening the upper water gates. Sam would have liked to be in Jem's place, driving two strong young horses at a spanking speed, but he was not used to driving from horseback. Jem clearly was.

Three-quarters of an hour beyond Lewistown, a bridge arched over the canal on its way to a ford across the river. Parson Golightly hailed the driver of a farm wagon passing over it.

"Greetings, Brother Rickert! Have you seen the Express packet?"

"Not I," the farmer called down merrily as the *Ark* emerged from under the bridge. "Why the rush, Parson? Did its passengers run out on one of your sermons? I always do say two hours preachifying is a sight too long!"

"Nonsense, Brother!" the parson bellowed back as the bridge and river ford fell farther and farther behind. "My auditors pend on my every vocable!"

After a moment's hesitation Cherry asked, "Excuse me, sir, but what does that mean?" She did not like to admit that there were words she did not know, but admiration and curiosity got the better of her.

"It means my listeners hang on my every word." Parson

Golightly answered solemnly, but his eyes twinkled. A gust of wind ruffled his white hair, and for a moment he looked like the picture of the wild captain of the ghost ship in the book *The Phantom Fleet,* not gentle old Parson Golightly.

"I must say," the parson admitted with a sheepish laugh, "if it were not so hard on the horses, I would be late to weddings or pursue packets at least once a week."

Now and again the parson's horses were rewarded with a half mile or so at a comfortable jog. At one spot, a boy fishing in the river reported that the Express had passed "a while back." The next lockkeeper guessed that it had cleared his gates "no more'n ten minutes ago." That news was the end of the comfortable jogs.

"Drive 'em like Jehu, Jemmy!" the parson roared.

Four miles farther on, a foot traveler answered Sam's shouted question with, "Pioneer Express packet? She just went 'round the bend up yonder."

First, they heard her horn signal the next lock. Then, there she was, dead ahead.

The twins gave a cheer and dashed to the front of the *Ark.* "We'll catch them even before the lock!" Cherry crowed.

"Maybe," said Sam, cautious as ever. "We'll come up to 'em there for certain."

The parson almost danced a jig.

"Hi, Jemmy!" he shouted to his grandson. "Let's see whether the dear dobbins have two minutes of real gallop left in 'em."

Yard by yard the distance between the two boats grew

smaller. Soon the children could make out figures perched atop the luggage on the cabin roof, then the hats and coats that marked their wearers as men, and the bonnets and cloaks of the women.

"Lookit that one there." Sam pointed. "If he hasn't got a fur coat on, he's surely fat!"

"Mr. Dickens!" Cherry was awestruck.

When the *Ark* came within hailing distance of the packet, a man standing at the stern of the passenger boat waved and then raised his hands to his mouth to shout.

"Two dollars says we still git to the lock first, Parson."

"Gamblin' is a sin, Tom Thatcher!" Parson Golightly bawled back.

"Use your heels! Thump harder, Jemmy," Cherry shrieked. "They're pulling away."

Sam gave a shrug and a sigh. "Bound to, I reckon. They always change horses reg'lar as clockwork. Theirs must be a good eight miles fresher'n the parson's."

To the parson's dismay, his horses were beginning to labor. Their heads tossed and then bobbed low as they lunged into their harness instead of pulling steadily. The race was as good as over.

"Pull 'em up, Jem, my boy!" the parson called. "No race is worth running a good horse down into the ground."

Cherry swallowed her disappointment. They could, after all, board the Express at the lock, or the village wharf beyond. And Parson Golightly would be on time to marry his wedding couple.

And she and Sam were about to meet Mr. Dickens!

* * *

As the *Ark* eased to a full stop at the lock to wait for the
Express to clear the lock chamber, Cherry was beside herself
with excitement.

"Oh, jiminy!" She brushed feverishly at her workaday
apron. "And us looking like we spent all night in a dust
bucket!"

"Cherry—"

"You'd best comb your hair, too. Drat! Where'd I put my
comb?"

"*Cherry!* Lookit *there.*"

"There" was behind them. Fifteen or twenty yards back
down the canal, a log raft had just moved away from the
bank, heading down-canal. A small man in a too-tight green
frock coat and old-fashioned flat-crowned hat sat on an up-
ended crate in its middle. The man pushing off with the raft-
ing pole wore a coat of the same cut and a shabby, tall hat
with a crooked turkey feather stuck in its band.

8

"Mr. Dickens's book!" Cherry wailed. She pointed. "They already have it!"

Sam leaned over the stern of the *Ark* to peer after the raft as it slid away down the canal.

"Where? I don't see any book."

"There." Cherry gave her brother a blow on the shoulder that made him grab for the rail to keep his balance. "The little man, the one sitting on the crate. He has it stuffed down in his coattail. Don't you see how it sticks out, all flat and stiff? Come along—we have to go after them!" She pulled at Sam's arm.

Sam was about to object when he saw the pudgy little man on the retreating raft pull a flat, booklike object from the suspicious-looking coattail, and start turning its pages back and forth.

"By jingo! They did get it!"

"Miserable malefactors!" Parson Golightly exclaimed.

He stared after the raft. Then, as the lock gates opened for the *Ark,* he remembered his wedding, and signaled to Jem. "Indeed," he said to the twins, "it would do no harm to keep a sharp eye on them until the *Betty D.* comes along and your father can lend a hand. I cannot delay—I must be off to do my happy duty ashore, but I shall ask the lockkeeper to pass a word of warning hereabouts."

The twins did not waste time crossing to the towpath, for the *Ark* was tied up on the opposite side of the canal, and the nearest bridge was beyond the lock. Instead, they took the narrow bridge that followed the bank on the inland side, away from the river. The track was as muddy from Thursday's rains as the towpath, and it was lined with pussy willows and black willows with roots to trip careless runners, but the thieves were not as likely to spy the children there as out on the open towpath. The matted branches of the winter-bare thickets made good cover.

Cherry and Sam slipped and slithered as they ran back the way they had just come in the *Ark.* Keeping the thieves' raft in sight through the willows was easy enough at first. The tall thief was not a good pole man. For every push that sent the raft straight down-canal, the next bumped her against the bank or sent her into a half spin.

"He's tryin' to pole her too fast." Sam panted. "Silly ox! You can't hustle a raft."

Slow as it was, yard by yard the distant raft pulled farther away. Cherry and Sam, after the first half mile, felt their legs grow heavier with every stride.

"Bridge ahead," Cherry wheezed at last. "We'll have to wait . . . and catch us a ride . . . on the next eastbound float."

The next boat heading down-canal appeared behind them before they were halfway to the bridge. The twins put on a last, desperate spurt of speed.

"It's Cap'n MacGilp an' the *Juniata Jewel*," Sam croaked.

Cherry reached the bridge first. She hung over the railing, waving her arms, too winded to shout.

Captain MacGilp gave a cheery "Halloo!" as the freight boat came within hailing distance. "If it ain't the Dobbs twins! Where's your pap and the *Betty D.*?"

Sam, still breathless, waved an arm on ahead.

"Drop aboard, then, young'uns," the captain called.

The freight boat *Juaniata Jewel,* drawn by two tall mules driven by one of the captain's hired hands, was traveling at a good, sharp clip. She carried a light load—deer and buffalo hides—and gained on the little raft yard by yard while the twins explained about Mr. Dickens, his book, and the thieves. Stout little Mrs. MacGilp and Runty Meago, the second hired hand, listened eagerly.

"Well, I declare!" Mrs. MacGilp exclaimed. "If that don't take the turkey-cock! And Mr. Dickens was on that Express packet what passed us coming out o' that last lock?"

Cherry nodded. "That's what Mam says."

"If we'd knowed, you might have got him to sign your book, Sairy," said the captain. To the children he explained, "Sairy reads a bit out of that *Pickwick Papers* to us after supper most nights. Runty here don't understand more'n half of it, but that don't stop him listenin'."

"Hits got a monstrous heap o' words to it," Runty said admiringly. "Mr. Dickens must have a mighty big noggin to cram all them words inside it."

"We're a-goin' to help, ain't we, MacGilp?" asked Mrs. MacGilp.

"That's for certain, Missus MacGilp." The captain peered ahead. "We ought t' pass them skunks's raft 'afore long, young Dobbses. After we hand you off to your folks on the *Betty D.*, we'll keep right on to Lewistown and stir up the law officers. They'll take care of the dirty rascals."

Cherry's face fell. Once back on board the westbound *Betty D.*, they would be kept out of all the fun. Sam looked glum, too.

"Or if we pass a packet on the way," the captain continued, "we can give them the word. Five or six lively gentlemen passengers ought to be more'n a match for your thiefs. Runty and me and Hobe out yonder ain't sprightly enough, or we'd have a go at 'em ourselfs."

"Hmph!" snorted Mrs. MacGilp. "There's six of us in all, MacGilp."

Sam gave the captain a hopeful look.

Captain MacGilp did not appear to hear. "What's afoot, Runty?" he called as Runty darted off to the prow of the *Jewel.*

"Ho ho!" Runty scuttled back, chortling. "Them thiefs? I know 'em! They ain't so far off now, so I took me a good, sharp squint—and I know 'em. The tall one's my Cousin Perk. Perk Meago. The fattish one's Sim Owlglass."

"Perk?" Captain MacGilp's eyebrows shot up. "Your horse-thievin' cousin? I thought he was in the Dauphin County lockup."

Runty chortled again. He might have gray in his hair and beard, but he was no taller than the twins, and when he giggled he seemed more boy than man.

"He's just out. But Perk, he don't know how to stay out of a pickle. He's brave, but he ain't got a speck more in his brain box than a bog beetle. That Sim Owlglass, though, he's got a real mean squinny-eyed look to him."

"We can take 'em, MacGilp," said stout little Mrs. MacGilp. She rolled up her coat sleeves.

Mrs. MacGilp was clearly an excellent woman.

"Mebbe so." The captain, however, did not look at all convinced that the crew of the *Jewel* could do any such thing.

In the meantime the raft, still several hundred yards downstream, was lost from sight behind a thick screen of trees where the river and the canal at its side rounded a wide bend. The *Juniata Jewel* followed, her mules *clop-clopping* along the towpath at a spanking pace.

When she came out of the bend, the canal ahead was empty except for a far-off freight boat.

The raft was gone.

"Keep aholt of your petticoats!" Captain MacGilp bellowed over the confusion that followed. "Don't get yourselfs in a hobble. She ain't gone. There she is, over 'mongst them willows."

The raft lay where the captain pointed, one corner dragged partway up the bank, under a drooping canopy of willow branches. The wooden crate on which Sim Owlglass had sat while Perk Meago poled was slowly bobbing its way on down the canal.

"They're gone," Cherry cried. "Where did they go?"

There was no sign of the thieves. Ahead, a ramshackle wharf perched on crooked pilings. Beyond it a rutted cart road skirted a field of corn stubble, then climbed uphill toward a cluster of farm buildings.

"Horses!" Sam exclaimed. "I bet they're after horses."

"That's it," Runty agreed. "Sittin' on a hoss would suit Perk a sight better'n polin' a poky old raft. Cousin Perk's lazy as an ox."

Cherry whirled to face the captain. "Please, Captain MacGilp, swing over. We *must* warn the farmer. 'Twouldn't be fair not to."

"Besides," Sam put in, "the farmer, he'll have a gun. He can round 'em up and take 'em off to the nearest lockup."

"And we can fetch Mr. Dickens's book back to him," Cherry finished triumphantly.

"That's the sperrit!" Little Mrs. MacGilp nodded in approval.

"Wal, only if you guar'ntee you'll keep clear of Perk Meago and that Owlglass," Captain MacGilp agreed unwillingly.

He swung the tiller, hard, and the *Jewel* moved out from the towpath side toward the sagging wharf along the opposite bank. As the wharf came close, Sam, and then Cherry, climbed to the *Jewel*'s side rail, and jumped.

Keeping to the cover of the woods, Cherry and Sam climbed toward the little huddle of farm buildings on the hill slope. Wet, winter-dead weed and wildflower stalks slapped at their legs. Under the wet carpet of leaves, fallen twigs and branches snapped softly at every step. The shadows deepened as the sky darkened with the threat of more rain. The cart track up across the fields would have been easier going, but it was too much in the open.

"Take care where you put your feet," Sam warned.

"I'm trying," Cherry grumbled. It was surprisingly difficult to slip like a silent shadow through the woods. In the stories Cherry wrote, Summer Moon did it all the time. Indians in stories always did. Cherry sighed. Perhaps, she decided as she trod on a hickory stick dry enough to make an exceedingly loud snap, only Indians got enough practice to be good at it.

Farther on, at the corner of a field of corn stubble, the twins came level with a large, almost empty crib for storing seed corn. They crept out to shelter behind it for a look around. Owlglass and Meago were nowhere in sight.

The farm had a neglected look. A lone hog rooted near the log barn, a few hens scratched in the dooryard, and the sound of an ax rang in the woods beyond the house, or they might have thought it deserted.

"Where did they go?" Cherry hissed.

"Wherever the horses are," Sam answered. "I see a rail fence along the bottom of that field above the barn. That might be the horse pasture."

Back under cover of the woods, the children made their way up the easy slope. When they reached the corner where the pasture's split-rail fence met the woods and turned to run uphill along its edge, Sam slowed. He jabbed Cherry in the ribs and pointed.

"There!"

About thirty feet straight ahead through the oaks and maples, short, round Sim Owlglass sat perched on a fallen tree trunk like a fat, green frog, and pored over the book in his lap.

"He really *does* have it." Sam gave a shiver of excitement, then looked around uneasily. "Where's Runty's cousin got to?"

"He's the horse thief. He must be out chasing up horses," Cherry whispered. She took a deep breath.

"They'll see us if we cut across the fields to fetch the farmer. So how are we to rescue Mr. Dickens's book from them?"

Sam swiveled in alarm. "Us? But we promised Captain MacGilp we'd keep clear of 'em."

Cherry did not answer. She bit her lip and thought. There had to be something they could do. The law officers alerted by Captain MacGilp might wait for the thieves and the book in Lewistown, but what was to stop Owlglass and Meago from crossing the river or riding around the town instead of through it? Cherry almost—but not quite—wished Pap were with them. He could waltz up with his deer rifle and take the book. That might not be as exciting as hatching plots or plotting tricks, but it would be a lot safer.

Sam nudged her. He pointed again.

Owlglass, perched on his log, peered down at the pages open on his knee, scowled, then turned the book around and scowled at it again. Closing it, he frowned at the cover.

"I declare, it looked as if he had it upside down," Cherry breathed in Sam's ear.

Sam nodded. "D'you reckon he can't read? If he can't, I'll wager Runty's cousin can't neither."

"Either," Cherry corrected.

"Miss Priss!"

Crouched in the underbrush, whispering with their heads close together, the twins did not hear a low "Hah!" some yards behind them.

They did hear the crashing in the undergrowth that followed it.

Perk Meago's long legs cleared the split-rail fence and carried him over the brush and through the trees at an alarming pace. The twins scrambled to their feet and bolted deeper into the woods.

The longer legs won. Two large hands stretched out to fasten on their coat collars.

"Caught ya!"

9

At Cherry's shriek of alarm, Perk Meago gave her a shake as if he were a terrier and she a protesting mouse.

"Shuddup!" he growled. "Shut yer caterwaulin' or I'll give you sumpin' real ter screech about. You too, snip. You yelp agin an' I'll bang yer heads together."

Meago hoisted Cherry and Sam roughly by their collars. Half hanging in their coats, they were hustled on tiptoe through the brush and leaves to the log where Sim Owlglass sat.

"Lookit what I found, Sim."

The short, fat man in the too-tight green coat and low-crowned beaver topper stiffened and stuffed the book out of sight behind him.

"Keep yer voice down, you dad-blasted donkey!"

Up close Sim Owlglass looked even more like a frog. He had pale skin, bulgy, heavy-lidded eyes, and a wide slit of a mouth. His dirty hair straggled thinly out from under his hat brim. He was much more alarming than the big, mournful Meago.

Owlglass scowled.

"What the divil's this? You go scoutin' fer a pair of hosses and come back with a brace of brats! You surely did come up a couple quarts short when they was dishin' out brains, Meago. I got no use fer brats. Go toss 'em in the canal and fetch them hosses."

"I'd have had 'em here already if there was any," Meago said sulkily.

"Hogwash! A farm this size has t' have hosses."

"The only four-legged critter on the whole blamed place that's taller'n a hog is a swayback old mule with a wheeze like a bellows."

"Blast!" Owlglass scowled. "Then I reckon it's the raft again. Wal, all the easier to tip them two in the canal."

Meago's long face screwed up into a grimace as he paused to think.

"I dunno, Sim. Mebbe you oughter quiz 'em a mite first. They was scrooched down in the brush there, a-watchin' you. Spies, that's what they are."

Cherry drew herself up. "We're no such a thing!"

"We wasn't spyin'!" Sam said stoutly. "We was—tyin' our shoestrings."

Cherry stared. Shoestrings? A dimmer excuse would be hard to invent. But then, perhaps dimness wasn't a bad idea. The dimmer they seemed, the safer they might be. *And* it might be just as well if the blackhearted villains did not suspect that the twins had anything to do with the canal. . . .

78

Owlglass grinned thinly, showing a row of brown-stained teeth. "Spyin', eh? That won't do. That won't do atall."

Cherry took a deep breath, and this time when she spoke, it was in a whiny voice that made Sam blink.

"Please, sir, we weren't—we wasn't tying our shoestrings neither. We was h-hiding."

She sniffled and gave Owlglass a woefully piteous look.

"We was?" Danger or no, Sam was so startled to hear Miss Priss-and-Proper using bad grammar that he had to cover a snort of laughter with a fit of coughing.

"Yessir. We—we figgered you was the farmer," he wheezed.

"The farmer!" Owlglass's scowl deepened. He brushed at his fine, tight coat. "You sayin' you took me fer some dusty clodhopper?"

Meago blinked. "You, Sim? Why, a fresh coat o' paint don't look smarter'n your new duds."

"I wasn't askin' you, you dunderhead. *I* know I don't look like no farmer, an' I reckon they do, too. They ain't sand blind an' feeble witted. So they got to be liars. Purty limp ones, too."

Cherry spoke up quickly. "Brother's just scairt. So'd you be scairt if the law was after you. They been chasin' us ever since we run away from the orphan home over the mountain. We thought mebbe you was one of 'em."

"Haw!"

Meago's long horseface looked gloomy even when he laughed.

"Haw! Us? That's a hoot! First time a body ever took us fer the hounds instead o' the foxes. Why, we—"

"Keep yer foot out of yer mouth, you whopping great blunderbuss."

Owlglass turned his scowl on the children.

"And you two raggedy muffins keep yer chops shut, too. I got to put my noodle to work fer a bit here."

Scowling horribly, as if thinking was as heavy work for him as for Meago, he chewed on his thumb for a minute or two. Then he reached around and stuck a hand in through the lining of the back of his coat to pull out the notebook.

"Take a gander at this," he growled. "This here writing— what's it say? I broke my specs a while back, so I can't make it out real clear. An' Perk here, he don't even know *A, B,* an' *C.*"

Sam and Cherry stared down at the neat, looping handwriting on the book's green cover. Cherry could hardly keep herself from dancing a jig. It wasn't Mr. Dickens's book at all! The inscription read:

Cap. Dan'l Fogo
Pioneer Line
Express Packet *Jefferson*
1842, Trip Log 2

The twins' eyes met. *Neither Owlglass nor Meago could read* —so they had stolen the wrong book!

Cherry closed her eyes. Clear as clear, she could hear Mr. Goodge's voice saying, "This here name is what you keep your eyes peeled for." The name might be on the front cover, he had said. She could imagine Mr. Goodge pointing out the name *Charles Dickens* on a piece of paper, then one skinny finger stabbing at the words.

Mr. Goodge surely knew that Meago and Owlglass were not the reading sort. Even so, he must have supposed that they knew the alphabet and would recognize the letters that made up Mr. Dickens's name. *They* certainly would not have let on that they did not know an *A* from a *Z*—not if Mr. Goodge had promised them money. . . .

"Well? What do them pen scratches say?" Owlglass snapped.

Cherry, busy thinking up titles, forgot about being slow-witted. "A Peregrination across Pennsylvania" would, she thought, make a tip-top title for Mr. Dickens's travel journal, but before she could say a word, Sam trod on her foot and spoke up first.

"We don't rightly know, sir."

"Don't know?" Owlglass glared.

Sam stood with his head down, toes together and heels out, the way Zack Mossbecker used to do when Mrs. Huffnagle raked him over the coals for throwing spitballs in class.

"We can't read 'em. Miz Shottle at the orphan home don't teach readin'—only them alphabetical rhymes. She has us recite 'em to visitors."

Cherry was surprised that cautious Sam should invent such a good fib, and was puzzled by it, too. Sam always had a reason for everything, but—

"Why don't she teach it?" Meago asked curiously.

"Because," Sam said, with a pointed look at Cherry that was as good as a nudge, "Miz Shottle says it ain't good fer orphans t' know more'n what's good fer 'em."

Cherry got the hint. It *could* be dangerous if the thieves thought the twins could connect them to a theft. Still—

Quickly she put her finger on the *C* of *Captain*.

"I know that's a *C,* mister." Pointing to *Daniel,* she said, "I think maybe this'n's a *D.* Like in the rhyme."

Standing with her feet together and her hands clasped behind her back, Cherry began to recite in a singsong voice. "Charlie Carter's cistern leaks, Dickie Dawkins's drawer creaks."

Sam doubled over with another fit of coughing. Cherry might take a while to see the nose in front of her face, but who else could make up nonsense rhymes as quickly as snap-your-fingers? And Meago and Owlglass had fallen for it. They were exchanging nods and winks, following the hint in the sounds of *Charlie-Dickie-Dawkins,* to *Charles Dickens,* exactly as Cherry had meant them to do.

"That'll do. Give that thing here."

Owlglass snatched the notebook and stuffed it back into his makeshift coattail pocket. "I'll cipher out the rest when I find my specs. Right now I got to decide what to do with you two sprats."

"Say the word, Sim. I c'n give 'em a good biff apiece an' drop 'em in the canal easy as punkin pie."

Owlglass snorted. "Like as not, they'd swim acrost an' slither right out. Or a packet'd come along and fish 'em out.

Word passes fast along a canal. Just what we don't need, you blockhead. Grab holt of 'em and foller me."

Half an hour later a steady drizzle was falling, and Cherry and Sam were still shut fast in the empty corncrib they had passed on the way up from the canal.

The spaces between the hickory rods of which the walls were made were not wide enough to slip a hand through, and the wooden peg that fastened the door was jammed so tightly through the hasp that no amount of jiggling would loosen it.

Sam tried throwing himself against the wall once more, but it only bounced him back as before.

"I'm *starved*." He groaned. "I can't bear it. Mam is likely frying up bacon for sandwiches this very minute."

"Don't!"

Cherry thrust her hands into the pockets of her apron and tried not to think of bacon sandwiches. She put her eye to one of the spaces between the hickory poles and peered longingly down the slope to the farm wharf and the canal.

Sam kicked at the stubborn door. "We could be out in two shakes if I had a pocketknife."

"Oh, no!" Cherry wailed.

"What do you mean, 'Oh, no!' Of course we could."

"No, *look*."

On the towpath down at the far bottom of the hill, two familiar-looking horses had come into view. They were driven by a small boy.

And followed by the *Betty D.*

10

Saturday Afternoon

In midafternoon the drizzle gave way to a steady downpour that drummed on the corncrib roof.

"Drat!"

Cherry glared out at the rain from between the close-set poles that were the bars of their prison. Disgusted, she plumped herself down on the farmer's last few bushels of seed corn and folded her arms in defeat.

A moment later she shot to her feet.

"*Ee-ee-ch!*"

Cherry pulled her skirt and apron tight around her legs.

"Rats!" she screeched, edging toward the corner. "There're rats under the corn!"

"Don't be daft." Sam was scornful.

Cherry glared. "*Do* something." Her voice still had a squeak to it.

"Do what? There's no rats."

As Sam spoke, one ear of seed corn shifted slightly and then rolled toward the wall.

"There! You see. *I* didn't move it. . . . What the dickens are you doing?"

Sam moved to the center of the pile of corn. He began to scuffle his boots through it, then stopped abruptly. Cocking an ear, he heard a small, scuttling sound that stopped almost as abruptly as he had. He poked one booted foot into the heap again.

"If there's rats, they have to get in somewheres," he said. "And if they get in, they have to get out somewheres. Ho, rat-rat, go home, rat. A weasel is eating your babies!"

A whiskered face with eyes like black beads appeared amid the ears of dry corn, almost as if its owner had understood. With a whisk of movement almost too sudden to be seen, its gray, long-tailed shape surfaced and with a scrabble of tiny feet vanished again at a point along the pole wall near the door.

Sam was after it with a bound. Peering through a gap between the poles, he saw the dark, gray shape go skittering off into the rain.

"It was so *big!*"

Cherry still clutched her skirts close around her knees. It was all very well for Sam not to be bothered. He wasn't wearing skirts. Like most boys, he wore his trouser bottoms tucked inside his boot tops. Not for the first time, Cherry wished she were allowed to wear trousers. Tessie O'Connell wore them. "Shocking!" Mrs. Dobbs said. Girls might—and on the canal usually did—do the same work as their brothers, but young ladies wore skirts. And that was that.

"The hole has to be here somewheres. . . ."

Sam dug down through the corn with his hands, flinging the ears back like an eager dog digging a hole. When he reached the baseboard where the poles were fitted into sockets carved for them, there was the rat's hole. The base of one hickory-pole bar was gnawed almost completely through, and that beside it halfway through.

"Hah!"

Two sharp kicks from Sam's boot and the bottom of the most-gnawed pole broke free. In a flash, rats forgotten, Cherry was on her knees at Sam's side and tugging with him at the loose pole.

The pole snapped off—with a crack like a rifle shot—at the point where it was nailed to a waist-high crosspiece. Like a second shot, Sam's arm was through the hole and groping for the peg wedged into the door hasp.

Like a third shot, the children were out the door. Sam paused only to push the broken pole back into place for the sake of the seed corn and jam the door peg back as well. Then they were racing down through the rain to the canal.

Cherry shouted as Sam turned right onto the footpath along the canal, heading westward.

"Not that way!"

Sam stopped, rain pouring from his hat brim.

"There's no sense keeping after them two. They've skedaddled off to Harrisburg with the wrong book, an' we have to catch up with Pap. The *Betty D.* must be at the next lock by now."

"I know that!" Cherry stamped her foot on the muddy path and both feet almost shot out from under her. She grabbed at a willow branch to steady herself.

"There's a footbridge over the canal along by the river ford," she called. "Besides, the fastest way west is to head back east to meet the next float."

So far as Sam could see, it was more a case of six of one and half a dozen of the other. He supposed what Cherry really wanted was to get out of the rain a bit faster.

To keep the rain out of her eyes as she ran, Cherry held her hands over her brows. When she did, the rain ran down her wrists into her sleeves. Not that it really mattered. Her coat was already soaking up rain as if it were a large, brown sponge. She would, she vowed to herself, *never* go off again without her rain cape. Not even on a sunny day.

By the time the children had backtracked half a mile, the rain had slackened. Soon it was no more than a drizzle. Better still, a long, squat freight boat was making its way up the canal toward them. Before it drew near enough for Cherry to make out the name on the prow, Sam knew it by its shape and its mule driver's hat.

"Huzzah! It's the O'Connells' *Rosemary O.*, and that's Pat. He told me his mam had it in mind to plug up the holes in all their old hats and then paint 'em so they'd shed water, and sure enough she's done it!"

Sam was right. The mule driver's hat, the hat on the figure at the tiller, and two other hats visible in the doorway of the stable cabin of the *Rosemary O.* were a bright, sunny yellow.

The twins cupped their hands and shouted happily, their cold, wet clothing and empty stomachs forgotten for the moment.

"Halloo the *Rosemary O.*!"

The two yellow hats in the stable cabin door darted to the boat's prow. One small figure waved wildly; the other climbed onto the roof-deck and raced back toward the stern. A shrill little voice carried faintly up-canal.

"Ma! Pa! It's Cherry an' Sam. Ma! Pa!"

Stout, cheery, red-faced Mrs. O'Connell sat in her rocker in the *Rosemary O.*'s noisy family cabin with baby Brian across her lap, and toweled Cherry's hair dry. Cherry and Sam, wrapped in blankets, sat on the floor at her feet and munched happily on thick slices of bread spread with butter and honey. Best of all, they were heading west again after the *Betty D.*, and at a good, brisk clip.

"Tessie my dear," Mrs. McConnell directed, "you keep turning them hose so the stovepipe don't scorch 'em. Martha Mary, bless you, put the iron on the stove to heat again, for surely it's dead cold by now. How are you thinking to dry even the collar of the poor dear's coat with a cold iron? And you, Bernie, fetch that teapot here again. I see two empty cups. And I'll have a wee sip more myself. Ah, bless them—here's Frank and Annie with that firewood. Now where were we?"

Sam swallowed the last of his fourth slice of bread, licked his sticky fingers, and took up the story of the day's adventures where Cherry had left off.

Mrs. O'Connell stared. "A stout little gent in a green coat, you say, and a tall lump of a fellow with a feyther in his hat? Indeed and it's Misther Simmons and that rascal Perk Meago you're talking about. They did pass us. But surely Misther Simmons is no thief! Why, 'tis but two hours gone since he was sitting in this very cabin, drinking a cup of tea with his little finger crooked out like a fine gentleman."

"They were *here?*"

"Not that Meago," Mrs. O'Connell said firmly as she folded her towel. "Captain O'Connell knows that Meago for a villain. He would not have him touch finger or foot to our *Rosemary O.* The dirty rascal had passed himself off to Misther Simmons as a raftsman, and on the fourth time he ran the raft into the bank, he tipped the dear man in the drink up to his knees."

Cherry gave a delighted giggle. Sam let out a gleeful, "Ha!"

Mrs. O'Connell frowned as she went to work with a comb on Cherry's damp tangles. "'Tis unkind to laugh at a poor soul's miseries, my dears. Misther Simmons declared he had never had such a journey!"

"I'll wager he hadn't." Sam grinned. "What did he want besides tea?"

"A wee nip of whiskey in it," Frank O'Connell whispered in his ear.

"Hush your whispering, Francis. I heard that. Many a

gentleman would say a medicinal nip is the very thing for a rainy day and wet feet," his mother observed. She gave her own teacup a thoughtful look, but then dismissed the thought.

"It was advice Misther Simmons was wanting as well as the tea," she explained. "He said he had made up his mind to riding on and leaving that Meago behind. He wished to know which of the farms thereabouts would have a spare horse he might hire."

"Or two he could steal," Sam said. "His real name is Owlglass, Miz O'Connell. The two of them stole a pair in Harrisburg."

"They never did!" Mrs. O'Connell's hands went to her plump cheeks.

"Ask Pap when you see him if you don't believe us."

Martha Mary sniffed. "I *said* he smelled too ripe to be a real gent."

"And they did steal a book," Cherry put in quickly. "We saw it."

"Not Misther Dickens's book? *They're* the two y'r pa told us about?" Mrs. O'Connell's eyes widened in alarm. "They never did!"

"That's what they were after," Sam said. "But they got Captain Fogo's logbook instead. Neither of 'em can read, you see, so they took it by mistake."

The seven O'Connell children—even baby Brian, who must have been astonished by the silence—grew suddenly still. Their mother's face flushed pink, then red, then purple.

"To think of it! Why, the filthy, prevaricatin' spalpeen!" She spluttered. "And him—him telling us he had found the book but lost his spectacles, so he couldn't make out whose it was to return it."

"You *saw* it?" Cherry darted a fearful look around the circle of O'Connell faces. "You didn't read what was on the cover to him, did you?"

Mrs. O'Connell blushed again. Cherry and Sam took her pink cheeks to mean that she herself did not know how to read. But then Martha Mary piped up.

"*Pat* did," she said proudly. "Pat can read."

Mrs. O'Connell began to rock in her chair so violently that its joints squeaked. "Bernie, go tell y'r pa he must come down. You can be minding the tiller awhile."

According to Captain O'Connell, the villains' raft had run hard into the canal bank just past Lockport, and tipped its riders into the water. Sim Owlglass—"Misther Simmons"—had clambered out a few yards from the spot where the *Rosemary O.* had tied up to change mules and drivers. He had cursed and shaken his fist at Meago. Then, finding his coattails dripping, he had pawed frantically at one inside coattail pocket, and pulled out a green stiff-cover notebook.

Captain O'Connell puffed his chest out a bit. "Pat, the dear boy, has eyes like a hawk and wits as sharp as your ice pick. 'How do,' says he. '*You* ain't Captain Fogo,' says he. 'And why should you think I might be?' says the gent. 'Because it's his logbook you're shakin' the drips from,' says Pat. The gent catches his breath, and he says, 'It's glad I am to hear it, for I lost my specs, so when I found the book on the towpath back a ways, I couldn't make out the name. And how do I go about finding this Fogo to return his wee book?' 'Well,' says I, 'we can take it off y'r hands if you like. We're headin' his way and you're not.' "

"And he gave it to you?" Cherry squeaked.

"Frank," said Mrs. O'Connell, "fetch the book down from the top shelf there."

And there it was: Cap. Dan'l Fogo, Pioneer Line Express Packet *Jefferson,* 1842, Trip Log 2.

"Where—where did he go after he drank up his tea?" Sam asked uneasily.

"Off to hire him a horse, says he," said the Captain, "and then on east, says he."

"West, Pa!" Bernie's excited call rang down the short passageway from the rear deck. "West! Mr. Simmons and that Meago, they just rode past. At a gallop. Durn near crowded Pat and the mules into the canal!"

11

Captain O'Connell held his battered pocket watch to his ear, then gave it a shake.

"Pish! Dead again. Alas, it's a sorry excuse for a timepiece. I was surely diddled by the peddler who sold it. No matter." He cocked an eye upward, where the sun was a faint spot of brightness in the cloudy sky.

"Sure and it must be well past three. But that's no matter neither. Let's see, now. If you're right, and 'twas midday when you saw the *Betty D.* pass your hill-farm landing, then with the one horse towing, 'tis certain sure she's beyond the next lock by now. We'll never catch her up, for we must stop there. 'Tis our terrible bad luck. The jenny mule cast a shoe this very morning, and we must have her shod before she takes to the towpath again."

"But we *have* to catch the *Betty D.*!" Cherry protested. "And then the Express—to warn Mr. Dickens before those skunks can steal the real book."

"If Mam don't skin us when we get back home for up and taking off without a by-your-leave," Sam muttered.

"Pooh!" said young Bernie. "I wouldn't fret. Your mum don't have the muscle to give a proper hiding." He cast a regretful look at his own mother, who had more than enough muscle for such chores.

Captain O'Connell sighed. "Sure and you'll niver catch the Express. Not now. She'll be in Hollidaysburg by"—he screwed his eyes shut and calculated swiftly on his fingers—"by four or five in the morning. Sunday or no, the passengers will be rising at six, and by eight will have thimselves and their traps aboard the portage railcars and be off and away up the mountain. Indeed, y'r pa and the *Betty D.* will be doing well if they reach the foot of the railway tomorrow nightfall."

Sam looked as worried as Cherry. "Does that mean the news can't reach the Express either—about the thieves, I mean?"

"'Tisn't atall likely," Mrs. O'Connell said. "Not even if y'r pa has tipped the word to ivery boat that's passed since breakfast. The fastest of 'em was the slow packet, and that only an hour ago."

A gleam suddenly lit up the captain's eyes. "Still and all, there's the *General Armstrong*! She's the only float on the canal as might do it."

Sam's eyes widened. "The 'Peerless Packet'?"

"The same. 'Tis her very first trip."

The Dobbs children had completely forgotten the new *General Armstrong*, the "Peerless Packet" due to begin service the day before. Shopwindow fliers and newspaper advertise-

94

ments had for weeks promised that she would be the fastest and most comfortable boat on the canal, and make the fewest stops.

Captain O'Connell, head tipped back and eyes shut, muttered to himself as he calculated on his fingers. "With no delays, Harrisburg eight A.M., Duncan's Island fifteen past ten, Mifflintown ... Lewistown ..." Captain O'Connell's knowledge of the Juniata freight traffic and the packet timetables was famous up and down the canal.

His eyes flew open. "Mount Union, ten o' the clock, P.M., arriving Hollidaysburg at about nine tomorrow in the mornin'. With a real bit of push she might make it by eight."

Cherry beamed. "Then all the *Betty D.* has to do is make it to Mount Union by ten o'clock tonight to catch the *General Armstrong.*"

Sam was not quite so cheerful. "*If* we catch the *Betty D.*"

Mrs. O'Connell perked up her ears.

"Ah, and indeed you may. Hush and have a listen," she said as Captain O'Connell raised his trumpet to blow the *Rosemary O.*'s *toot-tee-tee-toot-toot.*

A second horn blast echoed up the valley behind them. *TOOT-toot-TOOT—toot-TOOT-toot!*

Cherry scrambled for the stern and climbed onto the plank bench, the better to scan the canal behind them.

"That's Sir Billy's call!"

"Sam, it's the showboats coming! If they don't mean to stop the night at the next town, Sir Billy might take us on along to the *Betty D.*"

To Cherry's mind, surely no other show in the wide world

could be more exciting than Sir Billy McIlhenny's *Extravaganza: Comedy, Tragedy, Tableaux, Minstrels, Ledgerdemaine, and Acts of Trained Dogs, Monkies, and White Mice,* as its posters proclaimed. To ride even a mile or two on the same boat with monkeys and the beautiful Lady Callista McIlhenny would be more exciting than—well, *almost* more exciting than rescuing Mr. Dickens's book and having him shake her hand.

Cherry hung so far over the stern rail, craning for a first glimpse of the showboats, that little Martha Mary tugged at her blanket to make her climb down.

"Rules," said Martha Mary.

"Don't fret yourself," Sam said to Cherry. He gave a sigh for the dancing dogs and acrobatic mice. "Sir Billy can't help us. His mules have three boats to pull. They'll never catch the *Betty D.* in time."

As Sam spoke, the showboats, *Shakespeare, Mozart,* and *Molière,* tied together tandem-fashion and drawn by a trio of tall mules, inched into sight around the last bend. It was impossible to mistake them, for though they were too far off for even the sharpest eyes to make out the legend MCILHENNY'S PEERLESS SHOWS lettered along their sides in red and gold, the gold glittered gaily. The boats themselves were painted a bright white with brilliant blue trim.

Captain O'Connell gave a pull at the tiller that nosed the *Rosemary O.* toward the right-hand bank. "Indeed, we'll just be letting them be first through the lock. *Sla-a-ack!*" he bellowed at Pat, out on the towpath.

* * *

"Difficulty? I see no difficulty," boomed Sir Billy Mc-Ilhenny when he had heard the bones of Sam and Cherry's tale.

The showboat captain, splendid in his striped waistcoat, high collar and cravat, and *very* high coat collar, made a dramatic sweep of his arm. "No difficulty at all," he proclaimed. "Bobbins will harness up our relief mules. With four stout jacks to pull us, we shall overtake the *Betty D.* before an hour is out. It will be our pleasure—indeed, our privilege—to have a chance to be of assistance even at second hand to the celebrated Boz. He is a gentleman whose work we deeply admire!"

Lady Billy gave a sharp nod of her golden curls.

"And, my dear, if we were to keep on to Mount Union at full speed afterward, we could be there in time to set up for a show tonight. It's not," she explained to the twins and the O'Connells, "that we don't get good audiences in little burgs along the way, but when there's a basin with room to tie the boats up abreast and rig a real stage, we can do a sight more than sing and dance and show off the animals."

"There's not a show west of Philadelphia to touch us," Sir Billy said proudly.

It took a considerable time for the three showboats to pass, one at a time, through the next lock. By the time they were back in line, the relief team was ashore, harnessed behind the first team, and ready to go.

"The best of luck to you!" the O'Connells shouted as the three showboats slowly pulled away. Frank and Tessie and Bernie and Annie and Martha Mary waved until the *Rosemary O.*, too, cleared the lock and they had to return to work.

Cherry, atingle with excitement, was aboard the *Shakespeare,* but Sam, being more curious about the monkeys and mice than about Sir Billy and his wife, had boarded the second boat, the *Mozart.*

"Well now, Miss Dobbs!"

Lady Billy, seen close-to, was considerably older than her curls and ribbons and tiny waist suggested. With a flutter of hands she shooed Cherry toward the cabin at the rear of the boat. "Shall we have a cup of tea, dearie?"

By the foot of the steps leading down into the large, rear cabin, a stack of placards stood propped against the wall. In the middle of the cabin a stout, gray-haired female in a striped silk gown sat on the carpet, straining to reach her toes. Because Lady Billy had stopped on the top step to speak with the steersman, and because staring at strangers was rude, Cherry stared at the top placard instead.

McILHENNY'S PEERLESS SHOWS
PRESENT
Songs by "the Carlisle Canary,"
Mrs. Callista McIlhenny
and the Celebrated Tenor,
Sir Billy McIlhenny

The antics of Higgs's
DANCING DOGS
MIRTHFUL MONKIES
AND MUSICAL MICE

Ever-Popular MINSTREL MELODIES from
The Harmonians

TABLEAUX of Tragical and Other Affecting
Scenes from History

AND
Performances of *The Honest Highwayman,* a Tale of
Nobility and Courage,

Featuring Sir Billy McILHENNY,
Mrs. Callista McILHENNY,
Mrs. Sophia TUPPER,
Mr. Anthony PEPPER,
Miss Daisy EDGEWORTH,
and Master Simon SURTEES,

Or, Scenes from Mr. Shakespeare's *Julius Caesar,*
Mr. Knowles's *The Hunchback,* or
Miss Bulstrode's *Grandfather's Clock.*

"Ah, there you are, Miss Cherry," said Lady Billy, coming
down. "Mother, dearest, this is Miss Dobbs."
"Oh, bless me—me curls!"

The stout woman, who was the Mrs. Sophia Tupper of the placard, clapped her hands to her gray head with a small shriek of alarm, and popped nimbly to her feet. Snatching up from the table a wig piled high with a topknot and dark, ribboned ringlets, she clapped it on and at once was a fine lady.

"Pleased as punch to meet you, my dear."

The ladies were joined in a moment by Sir Billy and Mr. Anthony Pepper, who seemed to be the only other member of the little troupe. Miss Daisy and Master Simon, it was explained, were midgets who had played the children's parts, but they had been lured away to better-paying jobs in a circus in New Jersey.

No sooner had the kettle come to the boil and a cake tin been opened than Sam appeared, accompanied by a bright little terrier named Macready. By the time the cups were emptied for a second time and the last cake crumb eaten, the boat was slowing. William Higgs, the steersman, called a warning down from the deck.

"There's the *Betty D.*! Two hundred yards ahead—and dead in the water!"

12

Once the greetings and scoldings and explanations—and everyone's expressions of thanks to the McIlhennys—were done with, Captain Dobbs gave a gloomy shake of his head.

"It don't look good, Sir Billy. Meago and Owlglass passed us this last time about two hours past noon, on horseback. If they found fresh horses when that pair tuckered out, they'll catch up to the Express well before it reaches Hollidaysburg."

Sir Billy nodded his agreement. "Yes, but if they fail in that, I fear they, too, may think of the *General Armstrong*. Were they to board her as passengers, they, too, could reach the Portage Railway at Hollidaysburg before the Express passengers leave the canal to embark on their railway voyage over the mountain."

Captain Dobbs rubbed his chin. "About that, Sir Billy—I don't rightly know as we can make it to Mount Union in time to catch the *General Armstrong*. Our towrope got itself caught on a sharp snag when Merry had t' slack off for an eastbound packet."

"But we got it worked loose." Merry poked her chest out proudly. With the *Betty D.* left shorthanded by Sam and Cherry's disappearance aboard the *Gospel Ark,* she and her mother had been pressed into service. Their canal adventure was going to mean missing school on Monday, but she would have the most exciting excuse Mrs. Huffnagle had ever heard.

"Right enough, but it needs repairing. That'll take time. And there's the horses to change over."

"And Grinny's skinned knees to see to," Darsie piped up.

"He went down when the snag pulled him up short," Merry said. "The poor thing still has the shakes. He won't like walking the plank to come aboard."

Darsie scowled. Horses could be high-strung, and might like a bit of pampering, but they weren't poor things.

Captain Dobbs considered. "I suppose the best we can do is try to get word to the *General*'s captain when she goes by. 'Twon't be easy. With six or eight horses at the gallop, she'll be going at an almighty clip. Much too fast to put anybody aboard in mid-canal."

Sam heard that as he came up from the family cabin with the pocket knife he had left behind that morning. He and Cherry exchanged a look.

"If we *are* in time to catch the *General Armstrong*—" Sam began.

"Then Sam and I could ask the Captain to take us with them," Cherry finished for him. "We can tell him about the plot—and warn him if the thieves come aboard."

102

"Dear me." Mrs. Dobbs was doubtful. "I don't know . . ."

"Time enough to decide that when we reach Mount Union," Captain Dobbs said.

"*If* we get there in time," said practical Sam.

"Ahem!" Sir Billy cleared his throat. "If I might make a suggestion, Captain?"

"Indeed, sir, you may."

"Well then—if you will lend an ear, my good lady has had a splendid idea."

As the gap widened between the showboats heading on west and the stalled *Betty D.*, Captain Dobbs's voice boomed out to the twins one last time.

"Cherry gal, you keep both them feet of yourn on the ground, an' don't do anything wild. You listen to Sam now and again. An' you, Sam Dobbs, you stick to your sis like wax!"

"Yes, Pap," the twins chorused.

On board the *Shakespeare*, Cherry's eyes sparkled as she and Sam followed Lady Billy down into the rear cabin.

"Are we *really* to be in a stage play? Up in front of hundreds of people?"

Lady Billy smiled. "Dozens of them, at least."

Sam looked as uneasy as if he had been eating green crab-apples.

"Just so I don't have to speak any speeches. Not in front of a whole passel of town folks."

"It will all be quite simple, my dears."

Lady Billy sailed gaily across the cabin. "No speeches, only a ladylike scream from Cherry as Miss Lucy. And after the show, you must keep your costumes on. When the *General Armstrong* arrives, the captain won't shoo away two such respectable-looking young persons as I shall make you. And you may return the clothes on your way back down-canal."

At the words "respectable-looking," Cherry caught sight of her own smudged face and damp, stringy hair in a mirror on the cabin wall. She looked down at her muddy coat and boots, her bedraggled apron and skirts, and then at Sam. He was in an equally disgusting state. Lady Billy was right. The captain of the finest packet on the canal would be foolish to believe a tale told by such a pair of ragamuffins.

Lady Billy threw open the door that led into the shadowy cabin beyond. "Mama?" she called back over her shoulder. "Have you the keys to the costume trunks?"

Sam and Cherry stared in wonder at the Aladdin's cave the gray afternoon light revealed as Lady Billy unfastened the shutters on the cabin windows.

Garden greenery was painted on the low ceiling, and a golden chandelier with crystal bobbles hung amid a small flock of Chinese paper lanterns. A small forest of signs hung on the wall nearby. There were signs for the WESTWARD HO! tavern, the ROMAN SENATE, BANBURY STATION, and a dozen or so more—even a painted hand pointing off to the left that read TO THE PALACE.

"Goshamighty!" was all Sam could say.

"Look there!" Cherry giggled.

In a far corner two statues of females dressed in what

looked like foolishly flimsy nightdresses carried stone jars. They stood with their noses in the air, ignoring each other. Dusty trees and bushes were crowded in among stone benches, a golden throne, velvet settees, and pots of flowers. The children recognized a tall, jeweled turban as the one they once had seen on Bluebeard in a fairy-tale tableau. It was hung on the prow of a small rowboat that stood on end against the wall.

Cherry, even when she saw that the chandelier was made of painted wood and bits of ordinary glass, was enchanted. The flowers were made of starched cloth, the velvet cushions of painted cotton, and the statues and trees and benches and boat were wire shapes pasted over with paper, but she thought it all magical.

To Sam it was a great disappointment.

"It's all trumpery! A cheat," he muttered.

"Don't be a donkey," Cherry whispered back. "If Sir Billy bought real gold and jewels and statues, bandits would come and steal it all before he could say Jack Robinson."

That sounded reasonable enough to Sam, though on second thought he supposed that it would take a much richer man than Sir Billy to splurge on real gold and jewels in the first place—and real trees, even planted in tubs, would pine away and die in a dark cabin.

Lady Billy held up a strip of pink organdy.

"Perfect! This is the very sash for Miss Lucy!" Rummaging deeper, she pulled out another garment. "And these can be Master Percy's trousers."

Lady Billy added the sash and trousers to the dress and petticoats, coat and shirt, and shoes and hose she had rooted out of the same trunk, and carried the armload through to the other cabin. Mrs. Tupper was left behind to search for a bonnet for Miss Lucy.

"First, the mud," Lady Billy said firmly. "Here are the washbasin and pitcher, and you will find hot water in the kettle."

Cherry hesitated. "I *have* to keep my apron. To keep my book in."

Lady Billy raised an eyebrow at the dirty work apron. "Very well, but in that case Mama must wash and iron it for you. And you must not wear it onstage!"

"Capital!" Sir Billy exclaimed when, after a good scrub and a long struggle with what seemed dozens of tiny buttonholes, the twins appeared on the *Shakespeare*'s deck. "You are Miss Lucy and Master Percy to the life! A trifle tall, perhaps, but some nice touches of shrinking and cowering when the villain carries you off should do the trick."

In the next hour, taking it by turns, Sir Billy made a speech to the children about the thrill of "treading the boards" (by which he meant acting on the stage), and Lady Billy described the plot of *The Honest Highwayman* and the two short appearances they would make in the first and last acts. Mr. Anthony Pepper explained how the stage would be set up and the play advertised once the showboats reached Mount Union. Best of all, Mrs. Tupper cooked up an early supper and everyone but the driver and steersman sat down at the cabin table to potatoes that had been boiled in a metal helmet, sliced bread and cold ham heaped on a small, round Roman shield, and applesauce dished out onto their tin plates from a battered old iron pot.

At dusk, about two miles outside of Mount Union, the gentlemen set up a portable box organ on the small patch of deck at the prow of the boat, and Lady Billy sat down to play "Yankee Doodle" and "The Girl I Left Behind Me," while Mr. Pepper worked the bellows. After half an hour Mrs. Tupper took her place.

Sir Billy gave Lady Billy a big smack of a kiss on her cheek as she stood waggling her tired fingers.

"Bravely done, my dear! By the time we tie up in the basin, most of the valley will know we have come."

"How soon before I have to be this Master Percy?" Sam asked glumly.

Sir Billy pulled out his pocket watch.

"If we are moored fast by half past six and can hire an extra hand or two, we will have the stage rigged by a quarter past seven. Shall we say half past for 'curtain up' on *The Honest Highwayman?*"

Lady Billy shook her head. "Eight o'clock would be better. It is late, I know, but we could sell twenty or thirty more admissions by then."

"You are right, my love, as usual." Sir Billy bussed her other cheek.

Cherry and Sam, embarrassed, watched the lamplit windows of farmhouses slide by, and then Mount Union lights.

* * *

The twins, once the showboats had tied up at wharfside, did not stay to watch the bustle of preparations. Instead, accompanied by Mrs. Bowers, the lockkeeper's wife, they went in search of the sheriff.

"Sounds like a plot out of one of Sir Billy's play-shows," Sheriff Jackson growled when the children had told their tale.

"Nossir," Mrs. Bowers said firmly. "Sir Billy offered to swear on the Good Book that every word of it is gospel true. He had it from Captain Dobbs hisself."

The sheriff took his feet down off his front-porch rail with a sigh. "If Dan'l Dobbs says it's so, I reckon it's so. I'll go root out four or five good fellows to keep an eye out for Perk Meago and this Owlglass. We can set a watch out along the road west, and tuck the others out o' sight down by the canal basin. You youngsters keep your eyes peeled, too. If Owlglass and Meago show their ugly mugs, we'll get 'em!"

Sir Billy and Lady Billy had been busy, too. On the way back to the canal basin, the children and Mrs. Bowers twice passed men wearing MCILHENNY'S PEERLESS SHOWS placards on their backs and announcing to everyone who passed, "Show tonight at eight o'clock! McIlhenny's Shows! Tonight at eight!"

The boats themselves were transformed. With the *Shakespeare, Mozart,* and *Molière* lashed together side by side, the fronts of the forward cabins had been opened out, and their hinged roofs fastened upright so that the wooded garden scene painted on the three cabin ceilings made a backdrop.

Platforms fastened across the three prows made them into a single stage, around which a frame had been erected and red curtains hung. The footlight candles were lit, and Chinese paper lanterns were strung along the wharf.

The excitement of a showboat visit had already begun to spread. A small crowd of children and big boys had gathered to watch a terrier in trousers and another in a frill of a skirt dance to Mrs. Tupper's organ tunes. A monkey in a red jacket and pointed hat passed a tin cup to collect the children's pennies. Mr. Pepper, in his Wicked Uncle whiskers, sat at a little table off to one side, ready to collect the twenty cents plunked down by each of the grown-ups who appeared.

Backstage, Cherry and Sam found Lady Billy peering out through the curtains.

"Thirty-eight, thirty-nine ... forty," she muttered. "Ah, well, Monday will be better."

Promptly at eight o'clock, Mrs. Tupper, the organ, the dogs, and the monkey were whisked away. Then the curtains parted and out stepped Sir Billy to announce "That stirring drama of vice punished and virtue rewarded—*The Honest Highwayman!*"

Sam and Cherry watched from behind the scenes, as spellbound as the audience was by the tale that unfolded on the stage. They had to be reminded by a sharp push from Mrs. Tupper to make their entrance when their cue came.

Onstage moments later, young Lucy and Percy Westover were kidnapped by two masked men (Mr. Pepper and William Higgs) from the home of their rightful guardian, Miss

Sophia Westover. As the villains set about their dastardly work, Jeremy Wayman, the "honest highwayman" of the title (who was Sir Billy in a youthful wig and tight corset), watched from behind a tree.

Cherry and Sam, flustered to see so many grinning faces staring at them from beyond the lamps, almost forgot to cower and shrink from the villains who seized them. Cherry, when she remembered, cowered against Sam in a most pitiful and artistic fashion. At exactly that moment Sam's sharper eyes spotted what looked like a familiar crooked feather sprouting up from a hat toward the back of the audience. In his excitement he gave Cherry a sharp pinch.

Cherry shrieked.

Mr. Pepper, startled by so convincing a piece of acting, drew back a step, but then swept forward to seize and carry her off, followed by Villain Number Two with Sam.

"What was *that* for?" Cherry hissed once they were through the door painted to look like a garden archway.

"That Meago," Sam said excitedly. "I saw his turkey feather. They're *here*!"

13

Miss Lucy and Master Percy were not due to reappear on the stage until the honest highwayman rescued them and returned them to the loving arms of their true guardian. Sam and Cherry took their chance and slipped out for a closer look at the wearer of the turkey feather. Clouds hid the moon and stars, but light enough to see by came from the Chinese lanterns and from torches set in iron holders along the wharfside and at the corner of a nearby warehouse.

As the twins worked their way along the fringe of the crowd, only a few heads turned away from the wicked uncle's secret triumph as Jeremy Wayman was arrested. Those in the audience who saw the children nudged and pointed and whispered.

Sam, remembering the two horrid spit curls on his forehead, felt his cheeks burn. He tucked his chin down against his fancy neckerchief. Cherry patted the golden false curls that peeped out from under her bonnet, smoothed her flowered muslin skirt, and wondered whether being an actress might not be more exciting than being a story writer.

The hat under the crooked turkey feather *was* Perk Meago's. The horse thief, half a head taller than any of his neighbors, stood with his hands thrust deep in his trouser pockets and stared openmouthed at the stage. Sim Owlglass, his hat tilted down over his brow and his shoulders hunched up near his ears, from time to time darted a look right or left or behind him.

Or, once, straight at Sam and Cherry Dobbs.

The sharp, beady stab of a glance flicked past the twins and then back again. Cherry kept moving even though her knees felt as wobbly as a newborn calf's. She was thankful for the ruffled white poke bonnet that kept her face in shadow.

Sam swallowed past the lump that he suddenly found in his throat and scowled right back at Owlglass. If the clean face, spit curls, silk neckerchief, stiff collar, and scowl were not disguise enough, nothing could be. Owlglass's gaze jerked back toward the stage, where Miss Westover, outside Jeremy Wayman's prison cell window, pleaded with him to reveal his true identity to the captain of the King's Dragoons. Sam sauntered away after Cherry, hoping that he looked as cool as Master Percy in the flesh.

Cherry, scurrying ahead, found Lockkeeper and Mrs. Bowers, who were the next best thing to the sheriff. Mrs. Bowers could not tear her eyes from the tender scene on the showboat stage, but Mr. Bowers moved away from the crowd and bent to hear the children's excited whispers.

112

". . . right there, toward the back . . ."

". . . in the middle!"

"In the middle, toward the back . . ."

". . . Mister Dickens's book . . ."

". . . didn't see the book, but . . ."

Mr. Bowers, when he saw which two men the twins pointed out, gave a brisk nod.

"Well, now! They must have it on 'em somewheres. Them's the two Andy Whipple says was asking after the next eastbound packet." Stretching up on tiptoe, he spied Sheriff Jackson standing in the shadows off to one side, near the front. The lockkeeper worked his way forward with the children close at his heels. No one noticed them, for as they went, the red curtain swished shut on the first act of *The Honest Highwayman,* to great applause. Afterward, Sir Billy came out dressed in a blue coat, red cravat, and white hat to sing "Kathleen Mavourneen."

Sheriff Jackson did not turn to look in the direction of Meago's crooked turkey feather.

"Yup, I spotted 'em soon as they turned up. And you're likely right about Mr. Dickens's book. The short one has one mighty flat tail to that coat of his. Besides, it ain't likely they would be heading back Harrisburg way unless they have what they come for."

Sam gave Cherry an excited nudge. "Once they're caught, we c'n still hitch a ride on the *General Armstrong*—to take Mr. Dickens his book back."

Onstage, Sir Billy finished his song and the red curtain swished open on the wicked uncle pacing up and down in a garden. The sheriff stuck his thumbs in the pockets of his waistcoat and kept his eyes on the stage.

"I'll pass the word to my reliables," he muttered. "We'll scoop 'em up soon as the show's finished. Might rile folks considerable if we tried it now."

Reluctantly, Cherry and Sam slipped back the way they had come. There was nothing more they could do, and it was almost time for their great rescue by Wayman the highwayman. Back behind the curtains at the far side of the stage they found an opening in the red draperies. Parting them only far enough for a narrow slit of a view, they took turns at peering through at the audience. They had to abandon it for their brief rush onstage to be reunited with Miss Westover and to discover that Jeremy Wayman was really the long-lost younger son of Lord Fanshaw, and no highwayman at all. After Lucy and Percy were sent off to bed with loving embraces, the twins scuttled back to their lookout.

"By jing!" Sam whispered. "Cherry!"

Cherry bent forward to peer out through the slit.

"It's Mam! It's Mam and Baby Ellen and Pap—and Merry and Darsie!"

The twins spirits rose—and then sank.

"There goes our trip on the *General Armstrong*." Sam sighed as he combed out the hated spit curls. "Pap might say yes, but Mam won't."

Onstage, Jeremy Wayman cried, "At last, my dear!"—the closing line of the play—and clasped Miss Westover to his breast. Sam and Cherry did not wait for the red curtains to

114

sweep shut on the end of *The Honest Highwayman*. There was far more interesting work afoot than taking curtain calls while the audience clapped. Instead, they slipped out through the side curtain and onto the wharf. There they headed for the little knot of Dobbses, but then veered toward the shouts and sounds of a scuffle that rose from the center of the audience. All around, heads turned.

"Hands in the air, Owlglass!" the sheriff bawled. "You, too, Perk Meago. That ain't a broomstick Tim Bockey just poked you in the ribs with."

Meago and Owlglass looked around wildly. Their hands rose slowly as they saw the crowd press close on all sides.

"Who are they, Sheriff? Canalboat pirates?"

"What'd they do—hold up a packet boat?"

Sheriff Jackson waved the crowd back. "Tim, you go fetch them manacles hanging on the lockup wall. And somebody hand one of them torches over here."

As a torch came bobbing from hand to hand into the center of the crowd, he turned to look his prisoners up and down.

"Well, Perk," he snorted, "I never would have knowed you, all cleaned up and dressed so spiffy. What clothesline did you lift them duds from?"

"Farm over Millerstown way," Meago mumbled sheepishly.

"Shut yer yap," Owlglass growled.

Captain Dobbs pushed his way through the audience. "Make way, here. Make way! Ah, Sheriff Jackson, you have 'em. Good work. Do they have Mr. Dickens's book?"

115

The rest of the Dobbses, following in his wake, crowded around the captain and the twins. Sam tugged at his father's sleeve.

"Tell 'em to look in Mr. Owlglass's coattail, Pap," he whispered. "That's where he had it last time."

"Well, like I said before, that is a mighty flat coattail," the sheriff agreed with a tug at his mustache. Lifting the tail of the coat, he felt inside for a pocket slit, and drew out a notebook with a stiff blue cover.

Meago made a sudden snatch for the book, but Sheriff Jackson was just as fast. The pages tore loose from the cover, but in a moment the sheriff had it safe, cover and all.

"Now, what's this here! 'American Notes, C. Dickens'?"

"Land sakes!" Mrs. Dobbs exclaimed, hugging Baby Ellen so hard that the baby set up a squall. "Why, I never was so excited in all my days!"

Lockkeeper Bowers gave Sam and Cherry each a hearty pat on the back. "Seems these youngsters weren't dishin' out moonshine after all."

"Them two?" Perk Meago stared. "We never even seen 'em afore."

Owlglass turned his squinty scowl from Sam to Cherry and then back to fix it on Sam. From puzzlement the scowl shifted to surprise, and then fury. He lunged forward, but the two men holding him tightened their grips and hauled him back.

Cherry shrank behind her mother. Sam, edging toward his father, realized too late that he had lost the best part of his disguise when he combed out the namby-pamby spit curls.

116

"The orphings," Owlglass croaked. His wide-eyed, heavy-lidded stare was more froglike than ever. "It's them two blasted orphings we shut up in the corncrib! I *knowed* they was spyin' on us."

"Bet you didn't!" small Darsie piped up gleefully.

"No matter." Sheriff Jackson smothered a smile. "Here, Cap'n Dobbs, I reckon you'd best take the book. You're heading west, I believe. Mebbe you can—"

A faint horn blast from down-canal suddenly stirred the crowd as a breeze stirs a field of corn.

"It's the *General Armstrong*!" came a cry from down by the lock. "The *General Armstrong*!"

As the *General Armstrong* came into view Sam leaned his elbows on the stern rail of the *Molière* and gave a happy sigh.

The *General* surged up the canal, lamps ablaze in the windows down her long sides and around the awnings at each end, her fresh white paint and green stripe agleam, and brightly colored pennants flying. She was drawn by six galloping bays, their manes flying and bells jingling.

"Goshamighty, ain't she the prettiest thing you ever did see?"

"*Isn't,*" Mrs. Dobbs and Cherry mouthed at each other silently over his head.

"She surely is fine," Captain Dobbs agreed. "But if Tom Garrett don't slack off right smart, she's going to hit the lock gates with one almighty smack!"

"How long is she likely to stop here at Mount Union, Captain Dobbs?" Sir Billy McIlhenny asked.

"Only while she's in the lock. Huntingdon's her only full stop in this stretch."

Sir Billy nodded. "Ah. And do you propose to, um, give the notebook to the *General*'s captain in hopes that he may reach Hollidaysburg in time to restore it to Mister Dickens tomorrow morning?"

Cherry and Sam whispered together.

Captain Dobbs rubbed his chin. "I reckon so. There's a good chance Cap'n Garrett'll make it in time. Our good old *Betty D.* won't get there till well after nightfall tomorrow."

"Pap?" Cherry tugged at her father's hand. "Pap—what if the *General Armstrong* gets in too late tomorrow morning?"

Sir Billy raised a warning finger. "Exactly! This Captain Garrett cannot chase the Express passengers up the mountain on the next railway car. He must turn around straightaway and head east for Harrisburg with his new passengers. No, someone else must take on the task of placing those notes in Mr. Dickens's hands. Someone who can follow to the summit of the railway if it should prove necessary. I understand that packet passengers stop there for a midday meal."

"*We* can go," Sam said quickly. "Cherry and me—I."

Captain Dobbs cocked an eye at him. "It ain't an idea I much like."

Sir Billy's eyes twinkled. "Come, now, Captain! Two such resourceful young persons? Who better to place in the great man's hands the treasure they rescued for him?"

14

Late Saturday Night and Sunday Morning, March 27th

Cherry and Sam slept in their coats, rolled up in blankets among the baggage on the roof-deck of the *General Armstrong*. Only the fore and aft running lamps were lit. The night was clear, and when two bunks below were vacated by a gentleman passenger and his wife who left the packet at Huntingdon some time after midnight, the twins chose to stay above decks.

"All the gentlemen down there are coughing and snoring like a barn full of donkeys," Cherry had exclaimed after listening for a moment at the top of the short stair.

Captain Garrett, who had a bunk to himself in a tiny forward cabin, nodded. "Can't stand the racket down there myself," he agreed. He handed up a pair of blankets. "Wake-up bell at half past five, breakfast at six."

Sam slept soundly—Sam always slept soundly—but toward morning Cherry twitched and smiled, stretched and mumbled. In her dream she wore the Miss Lucy curls she had left behind on the *Shakespeare,* and Mr. Dickens was shaking her hand in gratitude for the return of his notebook. "I shall be forever in your debt, my dear Miss Dobbs. What does it matter if the cover is the worse for wear? Not a jot! If ever you should chance to visit dear old England, you must stay with Mrs. Dickens and myself. Must she not, my dear?"

Cherry never heard Mrs. Dickens's answer, for the *General Armstrong*'s wake-up bell clanged out merrily only six short feet from her ears.

Sam sat up first, and blinked at the still-dark sky. "'S it five-thirty already?"

Long swatches of light gleamed on the water on either side of the packet as stewards lit the oil lamps in the cabin below. Soon the captain, a dark shadow against the forward running light, appeared from his quarters. Climbing to the roof-deck, he strode back the length of the packet and, with a cheery "Good morning!" to the twins, joined the steersman on the rear deck.

"Williamsburg ahead," he said, taking down his trumpet from its hook beside the cabin stair. "We've made pretty fair time for night travel."

With the *TOO-it-TOO-it-TOO-it!* horn signal to the next lock ahead, the first gentlemen appeared from below to wash their faces at the basin set up near the cabin stair. Several climbed on the roof to stretch and yawn and wait for enough light to leap ashore for a walk as the packet slowed in its approach to Williamsburg. A steward came up from below to empty two chamber buckets into the canal, and Sam and Cherry, who had never been aboard a packet before, slipped below for a look.

The curtains shutting off the ladies' section at the far end of the long cabin had not yet been opened. In the main part of the cabin lanterns had been lit, for as yet only a faint light came from the windows along the sides, even though their red curtains were drawn and the green venetian blinds pulled up. In one corner a dozen passengers were lined up for a shave from the barber who had set up shop there. The second steward had already stacked the folded blankets into a neat pile and was unhooking the last of the thirty-odd narrow, canvas-covered frames that, fastened to the walls in threes, one above the other, and supported by a chain from the ceiling, served as bunks.

"Jiminy!" Sam whispered. "They look more like bookshelves than bunks. How do folks keep from rolling off?"

The steward bustled past on his way to a storage cupboard with the blankets. He beamed.

"Pretty nifty, ain't it? No benches, only chairs. Widest bunks on the canal. And Captain Garrett has us empty the spittoons and change the sawdust on the carpet three, four times a day."

"Yes, it's very nice." But Cherry wrinkled her nose at the sight of so many spittoons and the circle of tobacco stains in the sawdust spread around each one to protect the carpet. If gentlemen *had* to be silly and chew tobacco, why couldn't they practice to be sharper spitters?

121

"Breakfast in five minutes," the steward in charge announced. He and his assistant had pushed the three tables together to make one long one, and were setting out the contents of the larder cupboard: bread, butter, cold salmon, ham, and chicken. The aroma of coffee came from the tiny kitchen, where the cook was busy frying bacon, eggs, and sausages.

Up on deck Captain Garrett was at the tiller as the *General Armstrong* coasted toward the open doors of the Williamsburg lock. Before Cherry could ask a question, he held up a hand.

"Tush, Miss Dobbs, try not to fret. I believe we shall reach the Portage Railway in good time. We keep our first relay of fresh horses for the return trip here in Williamsburg rather than at the canal basin in Hollidaysburg. Five minutes spent on a quick change of teams now rather than on our return trip—I calculate that will save us upwards of half an hour."

Cherry, her heart thumping pleasantly, went to stand in line at the washbasin set up beside the cabin stair. When her turn came she splashed water on her face and dried it on the towel hanging on a nail there for the passengers' use. Then she set to scrubbing hard at her work-grimed hands. Nothing could be done about her dreadful fingernails, but her hands at least would be clean for shaking hands with Mr. Dickens!

After breakfast—for which the captain would not let the cook charge them the usual twenty-five cents apiece—Cherry felt under the collar of her coat for the needle she had tucked there and then forgotten. It was still in place, with the thread wound around it. Even though Mr. Dickens might say, as in his dream, that it was of no consequence, the cover of his notebook was in sad shape.

Fortunately, the cover of her own notebook was not only the same size, but the right color. Drawing *The Indian Maid's Revenge* from her apron pocket, Cherry took the piece of white bread she had saved from breakfast, peeled off the crust, and pressed the rest into the shape of a fat pill. With it, she began carefully to erase the lightly penciled title on her notebook cover.

"I need your pocketknife," she told Sam. "I'm going to switch covers so Mr. Dickens's won't look so dreadful."

Sam fished in his pocket. "He'll know. Your cover ain't as nice. And there's his writing, too."

" 'Isn't.' Of course he'll know. We're going to tell him all about it. All about *all* of it."

The distance from Williamsburg to the canal basin at Hollidaysburg was about sixteen miles. For much of the way the eight fresh towhorses worked at the gallop. Nevertheless, to Sam—and to Cherry once the clean cover had been stitched onto Mr. Dickens's pages and the stained and torn one onto her own—the next two and three-quarters hours seemed like six. For a good part of the way they traveled along slackwater pools formed by dams across the Juniata River itself. So near the high mountains, the water supply from the river and the streams that fed it was in many places too low to fill a canal. That meant dams to deepen the river, locks leading to and from the stretches of canal, and towpath bridges to carry the horses across the Juniata for the river portions of the journey.

Even Sam began to bite his fingernails.

Hollidaysburg—a town that still had a raw, treeless, newly built look to it—finally appeared ahead. The final stretch of canal skirted the southern edge of the town and ended in a wide canal basin. Its long wharves were furnished with many warehouses and slips, and in most of the latter, freight boats were moored.

Cherry and Sam, looking everywhere for the Express packet, dodged among the *General Armstrong*'s passengers, who were sorting out their luggage on the roof as the boat entered the basin. From his place at the tiller, Captain Garrett gave them a shout.

"Miss Dobbs, Master Dobbs! The Express! Over yonder." He waved his arm. "Fifth berth along."

So it was. But its roof was bare of baggage and no passengers were to be seen. A steward was drawing a bucket of water from the canal, and another was overseeing the loading of several baskets of foodstuffs from a grocer's wagon. Only freight cars lined the railway tracks that ran alongside the wharf.

Three minutes later the children were dashing down the wharf with Captain Garrett bustling along behind.

"The Express passengers?" said a railway-train driver in answer to their question. "Their train left half an hour ago, Cap'n."

"Philadelphia Smeal," the driver added as he shook Captain Garrett's hand. "Phil to everbody around these parts."

124

The captain nodded. "Mr. Smeal, meet two of Captain Dan Dobbs's crew. They need to catch up with one of the Express passengers, to return a valuable bit of property. To the celebrated Mr. Dickens, no less."

"You don't say!" Philadelphia Smeal made the twins a bow. When he had heard a bit of the story, he held up a hand. "Sounds as if there's no time to be wasted. You'd best come with me. There's two vacant seats on the tailboard of my last car."

"Mr. Smeal, sir? We don't have any money for fares," Sam said awkwardly.

"Don't need any. I don't take passengers. Not paying ones, anyway." Phil Smeal winked.

Just short of four miles up the valley the little railway train pulled into the hitching station at the foot of grade number ten on the famous Portage Railway over the crest of Allegheny Mountain. While the workmen unhitched Mr. Smeal's steam engine from the cars, Cherry cast a doubtful look up the long, two-track grade to the engine house almost half a mile away. Neither she nor Sam had ever seen anything like it.

"That rope pulls a whole train up all that way?" she marveled. The train's three cars surely weighed tons, and the rope to which the workmen had set about hitching them looked no thicker than a man's arm.

Mr. Smeal smiled. "Oh, once in a while one of 'em breaks, but most times they get 'em changed before they get too frazzled. No need to fret. There's a little safety car they hitch on the back. Works as a brake. Here, you trot up to the front end and set yourselves on the footboard up there. It's like a bench, kind of. It's safer that way goin' uphill."

Sam eyed the man who appeared to be in charge of the hitching station uncertainly. "He'll want us to pay, won't he?"

"Leave that t' me." Mr. Smeal gave him a hearty slap on the back. "I'll tell him about Mr. Dickins's book. And if anyone up top makes a fuss, you tell 'em Phil Smeal said you was all right."

Mr. Smeal walked the children up to the front of the rail cars, where Sam plumped himself down on the footboard. Cherry, trying gingerly to seat herself, clutched the skirts of her coat tightly around her bottom with one hand and pulled her apron around the frilly, bunched-up skirt of the Miss Lucy dress with the other, to protect it from smudges. As a signal flag waved from the engine house far above, and a moment later the rope began to move, the footboard gave her a sharp nudge that sat her down with a bump.

The freight cars jerked slightly, then began to rise. The twins held on tight. The motion felt very strange, for it looked almost as if the hillside were sliding away under their feet.

As the mountain gap narrowed, the children saw on the opposite side from the railway the old stagecoach road climbing its zigzag way through the trees to the summit. Its curves followed the slopes and ravines, while the railway grades were straight, cut deeply into the mountainside or crossing ravines filled in behind great stone walls.

As the cars rose, the children soon saw another train coming down on the track beside their own. The up train and down train balanced each other on the endless rope, and passed at the middle of the grade, almost close enough to touch.

The unhitching and hitching was repeated again and again on the journey up the mountain. From the top of each grade the cars had to be pulled along the level by a steam engine —or, as on the third level, horse teams—to the foot of the next grade. Sam and Cherry, as they waited at the foot of the last grade, ventured to the edge of the roadbed to peer back down the ravine.

"Jiminy! I wonder how high up we've clumb."

Cherry did not hear. Shrinking back from the edge, she pointed down the ravine and across to the stagecoach road below.

"Sam, *look!*"

Two tiny horses, led by two tinier figures on foot, were plodding up the winding stagecoach road. The shorter figure was in the lead; the taller lagged behind. Much of their way was screened by trees. It was impossible to be sure, but to Sam it looked as if the first man's coat was green.

He scowled. "It can't be them. It can't."

"It is." Cherry gritted her teeth. "It is!"

15

"But—"

Sam hurried after Cherry toward the railway cars. The look of horror he wore was one Cherry had last seen the time he found a big, ugly click beetle in his baked beans at the church picnic.

"It can't be them," he repeated. "How could they get away from the sheriff down in Mount Union?"

"*I* don't know, do I? All those people on the dock—it was very confusing. Maybe when folks rushed off for a look at the *General Armstrong* they just broke loose and slithered away."

As Cherry sat down again on the first freight car's footboard, she bunched the white flounces of the Miss Lucy skirt into a wad and stuffed it under her apron. She pulled her dark coat as close around the awkward lapful of apron, notebooks, and skirt as she could.

"Turn up your coat collar," she urged. "And—and pull

down your hat." Thankful that their coats were almost the same brown as the paint on the railway car, Cherry untied and pulled off her bonnet, then drew her head down inside her turned-up collar, turtle fashion.

"Don't be such a goose. They can't see us up here. The whole railcar's in the way."

"I don't care. I can feel Mr. Frog-Eyes looking-looking-looking a hole right through it."

Sam gritted his teeth. "They keep coming back. Like—like termites."

"Or mildew," Cherry said grimly. "What shall we do now?"

Sam thought for a moment. "We could tell the engineer up at the summit about Mr. Goodge and the book and Mr. Dickens. His crew could keep Perk Meago and awful Owl-glass from getting near Mr. Dickens or the packet passengers' railcars. They could catch 'em and tie 'em up and send 'em back to Mount Union."

Cherry shook her head. "Just because we ask them to? They won't. Not without Pap or Sir Billy or Captain Garrett to say it's all true. They won't believe it. *I* probably wouldn't. They would think it was all a tall tale. No . . ."

Sam eyed Cherry warily. He did not like the gleam in her eye. " 'No' what?"

"No, I have a better idea." Cherry forgot about being a turtle and sat up straight so that she could reach into the deep right-hand apron pocket. Her hand rested on her own notebook, in its secondhand cover.

"I think we ought to let them try to steal it again." She gave a dreamy look up the wooded ravine.

"Steal it again?" Sam stared. "That's batty!"

Batty or no, Cherry had clearly made up her mind. Once made up, Sam knew, Cherry's mind was about as easy to budge as Shade Mountain.

Cherry refused to explain. "I haven't quite got it all worked out," she confessed.

As the cars approached the crest of the mountain, the air grew colder. A thin mist grayed the oaks and beeches and hickory trees. The tree-clad mountainsides that crowded along the wide path cut for the climbing tracks drew back, and were shrouded in mist. Great shadowy rocks thrust their knees and shoulders through the grass on more gentle slopes. Here and there a ghostly oak or pine stood alongside the shadow of a split-rail fence. And then, a moment after Sam and Cherry heard the dim rumble of its engines, they saw the looming shape of the summit engine house. Like the four farther down the mountain, it was a broad, squat, four-chimneyed barn of a building, which the cars entered through a wide door, and where they were unhitched from the rope.

Suddenly, while the engine house was still little more than a shadow in the grayness, Cherry tucked her feet up under her and pushed herself up. Before Sam could stop her, or even be sure what she meant to do, she had edged to the far side of the footboard and jumped.

"Quick!" she called, running alongside. "Before the engineers see us and we have to take time to explain everything all over again. Jump!"

Sam grumbled, but he stood, and followed.

Together, the twins struck up across a grassy slope, and rounded the end of the engine house as their railway car slowed and passed through the wide doors into the darker shadows of the big shed. In a moment they reached the cover of a tall stack of hay bales halfway to the Lemon House, where the Pioneer Express passengers were eating their lunch. A steam engine and three railcars waited on the track in front of the Lemon House to take them the mile and a half to the head of the first incline on the way down to Johnstown. Some yards behind the train, a solitary freight car waited its turn.

"Why the all-fired hurry?" Sam panted. "It'll be a good ten, fifteen minutes before Perk Meago and the Frog can make it up here dragging their hosses behind them."

"We might miss Mr. Dickens—or not have time to tell him about Mr. Goodge." Hurriedly unbuttoning her coat, she handed it to Sam to hold while she pulled off her work apron and, setting it atop a hay bale, tried to fluff up the Miss Lucy dress's ruffles.

"I have it all figured out," she said briskly. Her eyes sparkled. "We'll tell Mr. Dickens everything. Then he can lock the real book away somewhere safe in the railway car and leave the other notebook out as if we had only just returned it. *Then,* you see, when they steal it again, the passengers can capture them. They can tie them up, and hand them over to the law officers down in Johnstown."

Sam frowned. Cherry was always a great one for complicating things. "Why do you have to give him your book? Why not use the real one for the trap?"

Cherry's eyes widened. "In case they should get away with it after all, of course. Mr. Dickens's would still be safe."

"Umph!" Sam snorted. "I don't s'pose it might be so you'll have to fetch your storybook back? So we'll have to ride down to Johnstown *with* 'em, would it?"

Cherry snatched back her coat and pulled it on. "I expect you have a better plan."

"Why not give Mr. Dickens his book, tell him about old Goodge, and let him keep the book safe so they *don't* get it?"

"But—" Cherry's chin lifted. "They would keep on trying. And"—she fished for a stronger argument—"and not getting it might give them such conniption fits that they might forget what Mr. Goodge said about not knocking Mr. Dickens over the head for it."

That, Sam supposed, was possible. He still grumbled. "You always have to have everything as twisty as a lanyard knot."

Cherry pulled her own notebook in its torn, "new" cover from the apron pocket and tucked it under her arm while she felt for the other pocket.

Sam was suddenly struck by a new thought. He was not sure whether to grin or to groan.

"You'd like to bend Mr. Dickens's ear all the way down to Johnstown, wouldn't you? Maybe wheedle him into reading one of your stories about that silly Summer Moon? That's it, ain't it?"

132

Cherry strode off toward the Lemon House with a dignified gait. Sam sighed and followed.

Cherry was only yards from the side gate to Mr. Lemon's front garden, with Sam at her heels, when they heard the muffled sound of hoofbeats on a muddy road.

Cherry wheeled.

"I still say it can't be them," Sam said, but he was uneasy. "Their hosses were played out more'n half a mile down the mountain."

He spoke too soon. The hoofbeats came pounding up through the mist that hung over the mountaintop, and on along the stagecoach road that passed to the west of Mr. Lemon's house and outbuildings. Two horsemen jumped the rail fence, swept down the grassy slope and around the outbuildings, and made a dead set at the twins.

Sim Owlglass came first, elbows flapping.

"Hit's them!" Owlglass crowed. "I told you so when I spied that bonnet peerin' down the mountainside. I'd know that there bonnet on a dark day in Hades!" He cackled. "Scoop 'em up an' foller me."

Perk Meago slid from his saddle and lunged for the twins.

Neither Sam nor Cherry had a chance to reach the gate. Sam tried to push Cherry ahead of him, but a large hand clapped over his mouth before he could so much as yelp. Meago's other hand caught Cherry in the middle of drawing breath for an earsplitting shriek.

Not a soul chanced to look out at one of the Lemon House windows to see the big man tuck one breathless twin under each arm and lope after Owlglass, leaving his sweaty horse to nibble on the shrubbery by the garden fence.

Owlglass dismounted across the railway tracks and out of sight behind the waiting passenger cars.

"Put 'em down."

Meago dumped the children as if they were two sacks of potatoes. "You was right, Sim. Here's that book." He plucked the notebook from Cherry's hand and passed it to his companion.

"That's the ticket!" Owlglass peered at the cover, then fingered the hasty stitches at the top and bottom of the spine. "The brat's patched it up fer us, too."

"How—how'd you get here so fast?" Sam panted. It didn't make sense. Their horses were sweaty and tired, but neither had worked up a real lather.

Cherry, for a change, kept mum. She still had a fast hold on the apron with Mr. Dickens's real notebook in the pocket. It was hard not to look down at it. She was frightened that she might bump it against something, or even attract attention to it with a nervous twitch.

Owlglass grinned a snaggletoothed grin. " 'So fast'? I calc'late that means you spotted us footin' it up the gap road. You figgered the hosses was blown, did you? Well, they wasn't! We was nursin' 'em all the way up just so's they'd have some puff left in case 'twas needed. Then we spotted that there bonnet."

Perk Meago scratched his head. "What d'we do with 'em now, Sim?"

"Wal, we ain't gonter take a chance on them comin' up

behind us agin after we light out fer Harrisburg, you lummox." Owlglass squinted at the children, and then at the solitary freight car. "Maybe we got us the answer right here to hand. You still got that bit o' wire in yer pocket, Perk?"

Cherry gave the door of the railcar another furious kick. The fastenings on both doors were tightly wired shut.

"Twice! How could we let them catch us *twice?*"

Sam was working to make a peephole. There was barely light to see by, but he had found a knot in one of the boards in the car's wall. Prying away with his pocketknife, he snorted.

"I reckon because you're not that Summer Moon and I'm not Natty Bumppo."

Cherry stuck out her tongue at him in the dark.

Still, Sam had a point. Summer Moon and Mr. James Fenimore Cooper's storybook hero, Natty Bumppo, were good noticers. They would have known that Owlglass and Meago were not walking their horses up the mountain because they had already run them too hard uphill. They would have noticed even from a distance that the horses picked up their hooves briskly as they walked, and walked at the men's sides, not pulling back on their halters.

Cherry drew Mr. Dickens's notebook from the apron pocket and spread the apron itself over the top of a small barrel—the car's cargo of crates and barrels had the smell of cheese and salt fish—and sat down on it to think. Or to cry. She couldn't decide which.

"There!" Sam announced as the knothole dropped to the

135

floor and rolled away. The light from the opening was dim, but it was better than none.

He put his eye to the peephole. "Shoot!" he exclaimed. "Here, come look."

Cherry edged past a stack of crates stenciled MESSRS. WALSH & JOHNSTON, JOHNSTOWN, and set her eye to the peephole.

Not forty yards away through the mist, the Express passengers were hurrying from the Lemon House to board their cars. Ten, twenty ... there appeared to be nearly fifty of them. One gentleman, in a handsome, high-collared fur coat, strode out with a lady on his arm, followed closely by two other gentlemen and another lady.

"Mr. Dickens!" Cherry cried. *"Mr. Dickens!"*

Sam began to bang on the car door and shout, and Cherry quickly joined in. "Help! In the freight car! We're locked in the freight car!"

No one heard. The steam engine to which the passenger cars were hitched blew a long, shrill blast on its whistle. No sooner had the last passenger vanished from the children's line of sight and the whistle died away, than a train of four freight cars came clattering down the eastbound track alongside Sam and Cherry's car. It stopped with a squealing of brakes.

Once the noise had died away, they set up their clamor again. The passengers and their train might be gone, but surely there were workmen not far off.

If there were, none came.

Cherry's and Sam's fists soon ached from banging. Then,

suddenly, as they stopped to catch their breath to shout again, their own car lurched.

Cherry darted to the peephole, but could see nothing but the cars at rest on the other track. "I think we've been hooked to an engine," she said anxiously. "We have to *do* something. What should we do?"

The car began to move slowly forward.

"Nothing," Sam said. He began to feel along the boards on the other side of the car in search of a north-facing knot. "I think we're on our way down to Johnstown."

The twins looked at each other, Cherry blankly, Sam wryly.

Then they laughed.

Cherry's eyes shone. "We *will* be there before Mr. Dickens leaves on the Pittsburgh packet. I know we will!"

She hugged the blue notebook to her chest.

16

At the engine station at the head of the railway's first downward grade there were workmen to spare, but the children kept as still as mice.

"What if," Cherry asked anxiously as they began to move again. "What if we don't reach Johnstown before the packet leaves for Pittsburgh? We *have* to return Mr. Dickens's book."

She was clearly worried, but Sam thought he detected a suspicious touch of hopeful excitement, too.

"The law officers can see to that," he said quickly as he pried loose his second knothole.

"Yes, but—"

Sam began to be alarmed. There was no telling how far a bee in her bonnet might drive Cherry. A trip over the mountain to Johnstown was one thing. Pittsburgh was quite another. As for Cincinnati and St. Louis, where the river boats went from Pittsburgh—they were on the edge of the Far West! Indian country.

"Don't you start fancifyin' again!" he exclaimed. "Even if we hand the book over to the nearest law officer and catch the very next train back up the mountain, we'll be in luck if we reach Hollidaysburg before the *Betty D.* does. About ten in the evening. That's what Pap said."

"I know." Cherry looked the picture of primness and patience. "But Pap said the Dobbses would do everything we could to return the book. And we *could*—"

Sam's voice rose. "We could *not*. First off, the captains on the Western Division boats don't know Pap. And we don't know so much as a stray dog down in Johnstown. Let alone Pittsburgh. Without somebody to say we aren't just spinnin' moonshine about the book being Mr. Boz's, a packet captain'll just say, 'That'll be two dollars apiece, please.' And what about all the twenty centses we don't have for breakfasts and dinners and suppers?"

"I suppose so . . ." Cherry agreed vaguely.

The downward journey was miles longer than the climb up the eastern side of the mountain, and the inclined planes not so steep. Even so, the views out through the knotholes were exciting. Sam and Cherry took turns at each side of the car, watching forest and streams—and upward-bound railcars—slide past. Now and again in a valley below they could spy a scattering of log cabins or plank houses, green pastures dotted with miniature cows, dogs running and children waving. Once or twice a farmer and his mules plowed a dusty green field brown. Other fields, half-plowed, stood waiting for Sunday to pass and workaday Monday to come.

"It's like flying," said Cherry breathlessly. "Like seeing what birds see."

Sam was almost more interested in what he couldn't see. Some way along the much longer level that followed the fourth downward stage, the changed sound of wheel upon rail made him strain to see more. They must be rolling across a stone bridge. A *high* stone bridge. The wilder scenery—steep hillsides and a deep ravine—made that clear. From below it must look as if they were sailing along sky-high! Just as interesting was the plunge several miles farther on into sudden, echoing darkness. Sam had read about tunnels. He had never been in one. The only trouble was, it seemed it would never end.

And then, almost as suddenly, they were out in the open and slowing for the engine house at the top of the last inclined plane. After being unhitched at its foot, the car sailed along at a great clip, almost as if it had been set loose on the gentle slope with no engine and no brakes. Through the north-side peephole Cherry saw the banks of a rushing river. Sheds and a house or two on the opposite hill whisked by.

"I see three, four houses," Sam announced from the south-side peephole. "No, more—and a church. *Oops!*"

Unexpectedly, the tracks had divided. All Sam could see was town, but from Cherry's side the river vanished as the car swerved away from its banks to run, slowing as it went, along the back side of the warehouses and slips of a canal basin.

Cherry gave up her place on the canal basin side to Sam.

"Look! We're there—we really are!"

Within minutes workmen came to unhitch and move the car, and this time the twins' thumping and shouting brought results. The warehousemen answered, and in no time at all one had untwisted the wire that held the door hasp fast.

"Well, I'll be blessed—kids! Now, how'd you two come to get yourselves shut up in there?"

"Please," Cherry said breathlessly. "How long ahead of us did the passengers for the Pittsburgh packet get here?"

"How long ahead?" The man took off his cap and scratched his head in puzzlement. "Well, if y' want to be partickler, I'd say maybe a second or two."

Sam leaned out of the open door for a look around. Two passenger cars and a baggage car stood in line on the track immediately ahead.

"Jiminy! We were hitched to them all the time!"

Cherry scrambled down. "Who are those people? Where are the passengers from over the mountain?"

A stream of gentlemen and ladies had appeared from around the corner of the farthest warehouse, and were hurrying to board the cars. The children, as their freight car was pushed off onto a siding, saw a steam engine come coasting down the track to brake to a stop in front of the passenger

141

cars. Their train *had* come down from the foot of the last incline without an engine!

"Those? They're the folks from the Leech's packet out of Pittsburgh. The captain hustled your train's folks down to his wharf right off. He—"

Sam and Cherry were already running down the line, past the row of boat slips and warehouse wharves. But as they rounded the corner of the big warehouse of the Reliance Freight Boat Line at the end of the basin, they saw only an empty packet-boat slip.

The packet *William Pitt* had moved out from the wharf and was making a slow turn westward toward the canal entrance. A number of passengers watched their boat's progress from the forward deck or the roof-deck. Others hung out of the open windows.

The children saw no gentleman in a fur coat among them.

"Mis-ter Dickens!" Sam shouted.

Cherry waved the blue notebook wildly. "Mr. Dickens!"

Several passengers looked back as the packet moved slowly toward the overhead bridge by which the horse teams crossed to the towpath. One man cupped a hand to his ear. "Who?"

Cherry and Sam ran along the street that followed the line of the canal. "Please," Cherry called. "This is Mr. Dickens's book!"

The steersman turned the tiller just enough to swing the stern of the boat closer to the bank.

"The English gent? He's below," the steersman said. "He

said how he'd set it down somewheres and couldn't find it. Here, hand it over, and we'll give it to Cap'n O'Meara to pass along to him."

"But it was—" Cherry hesitated as a passenger at the rail stretched out a long arm. Reluctantly, with Sam holding fast to her other hand, she reached out to pass the book to him.

Then it was out of reach, and the packet with it.

"But—" Cherry whispered.

The children hung over the rail of the overhead bridge and watched until the packet vanished into the aqueduct that carried the canal over the Little Conemaugh River.

Cherry sighed. "I do wish I'd gotten to shake his hand."

Sam thrust his hands into his pockets. "I have three pennies. If we can find a bakery we can buy some bread rolls," he said gruffly. "I'm near starving."

"It's Sunday. All the shops are shut," Cherry reminded him with a sniff. Trust Sam to think of his stomach! She stalked down the bridge ramp and off to wait for the next train up the mountain.

17

Sunday Afternoon and Evening

It was a piece of great good luck that, as the twins dashed up, the last piece of baggage was just being loaded on the baggage car which their freight car had followed down the mountain. It was almost as if the train were waiting for them.

To Sam's considerable relief, Mr. Philadelphia Smeal's name was as good as silver dollars to the engine driver and to the railwayman who was counting heads. That gentleman waved Sam and Cherry toward the platform at the end of the near passenger car.

"Lucky for you we're runnin' a bit late all around today, and that we're sendin' the cars up for these folks even though it will be dark before they reach t'other end." He smiled. "Phil Smeal's name may be good with us, but 'twouldn't have bought you beds for the night at McConnell's Hotel! Hup you go, there. We'll be off before you can say Jack Robinson."

The children found seats side by side just inside the car's

rear door and spent the whole of the upward journey trading chances to press their faces to the window. Sam found the tunnel much less alarming this time, and that he had been right about the high bridge they had crossed. Now and again the late afternoon sun broke through the clouds and washed the rolling hills with gold. Cherry, who had been all sighs and droopy shoulders for the first few miles out of Johnstown, almost bounced on her seat. She clasped her hands and drew in her breath to hold it in delight at the bird's-eye views of little houses dotted in clearings far down the mountainside. Their peephole views on the way down were nothing compared to these.

Adding a puzzle to all the marvels, after the cars reached the level at the top of the fourth upward plane, the driver of the engine to which their little train was being hitched came back along the cars, calling, "Dobbs? Dobbs? Any youngsters name of Dobbs in there?" When Cherry, nodding violently, knocked on the window, he mounted the steps to the rear platform and stuck his head in at the door. Seeing Sam's worried look, he grinned a grin as wide as his bushy red mustache.

"No fear, boy. I shan't turn ye out to walk." He winked. "The word come over the mountain to keep an eye out fer a pair of short Dobbses. If ye wasn't in with this 'ere bunch, we was going to have to send a car down special."

Then, with a second wink more mysterious than the first, he ducked out again to trot on forward to his engine.

The other passengers, as mystified as the twins, soon

coaxed from them the tale of the whole adventure. When, at the top of the fifth plane, the driver of the engine that was to take the cars along to the Lemon House came back with the same call for "Dobbs? Dobbs?" and no explanation once he found the children, the passengers' excitement and interest grew.

"It's likely only our pap and mam fretting about us, and Mr. Smeal helping," Sam said. He was uncomfortable at so much attention.

"Mam and Pap won't be in Hollidaysburg before ten o'-clock tonight," Cherry reminded him.

"Then Sir Billy. Or Cap'n Garrett."

Cherry shook her head. "The showboats are still in Mount Union. And the *General Armstrong* is likely *back* to Mount Union by now."

"Then it had to be Mr. Smeal all by himself," Sam declared. "If he got back to Hollidaysburg before the *General* left, I reckon Cap'n Garrett, knowing Pap as he does, might have asked Mr. Smeal to keep track of us."

"I don't think so," said a whiskered gentleman in a brown greatcoat with a fur collar. "If this Smeal is only a driver, I doubt that he could have ordered up the special car that first engine driver spoke of."

"Oh!" trilled a lady passenger wearing a blue velvet poke bonnet atop her heap of crimps and curls. "I do love a mystery!"

Cherry, who had been about to say that she loved mysteries more than almost anything, held her tongue. Not even the

146

admiring glances a number of the gentlemen gave the curls and blue eyes under the blue bonnet were worth sounding like such a silly goose.

At the Lemon House, the Lemons were not accustomed to having passengers to feed at suppertime, but they were ready with ham sandwiches, large pots of coffee, and spice cake. Because of the rush to get the cars as far down the mountain as possible while there was still daylight, Mrs. Lemon and her helpers carried the food out to the cars in baskets. To Sam's huge relief, several passengers got together to pay for suppers for Cherry and Sam.

Better still, several passengers did not claim their second sandwiches or portions of cake. Sam, nearly cross-eyed with hunger after missing lunch, put away three thick sandwiches and two cups of coffee. Left with no room for cake, he tore two wide strips from an abandoned Pittsburgh newspaper and wrapped a piece of cake in each, for stowing in his coat pockets. Cherry polished off a sandwich with her coffee, and then three slices of cake.

On the ride down the gap, the darkening shadows made the mountains above seem even higher, the slopes steeper, and the ravine below deeper than they had been in the morning. On the last part of the journey it became all too clear why the Portage Railway was, as a rule, shut down before nightfall. Had it not been for the lanterns glimmering at the hitching shed below, riding down the last grade would have been very like sliding into an inkwell.

"I hope the rope don't break," Sam muttered.

"Doesn't." Cherry picked the last crumb of cake from her apron and kept a nervous watch out into the blackness on the ravine side.

To the twins' delight, Philadelphia Smeal stood waiting alongside the tracks at the foot of the grade. A second figure, with half a dozen lanterns lined up at his feet, stood nearby. As the cars were being unhitched from the rope cable, Mr. Smeal, lantern in hand, climbed to the front platform of the children's car and stuck his head in at the door.

"'Evening, young Dobbses." He grinned. "I'm right glad t' see you two. Thought I'd best bring up extry lanterns fer the ride down t' town."

At the children's question about the drivers above who had been on the lookout for Dobbses, his eyebrows shot up like upside-down **V**'s.

"Wal, I don't rightly know. Howsomever, it could be that the tale o' your chase after those book thieves got passed along. I told some folks on their way up to Sam Lemon's. They'll have passed it along, I reckon." He handed the lantern to the tall gentleman with the fur collar. "There's a hook fer this up in the middle of the ceilin' yonder."

With a hasty nod, he bustled away to see to his horses.

Cherry frowned. "*He* was in a hurry."

Sam shrugged. "It's late." He yawned.

The reason for the extra lanterns was soon all too clear when the cars headed down the track to Hollidaysburg—

148

without horses or engine. The track was almost level, but not quite. After a snail's-pace start, they gathered speed and soon were rolling along at a merry clip. Mr. Smeal and his companion, standing one on each side of the front platform, swung their lanterns from side to side and from time to time gave shouts of warning to livestock—and deer—that strayed too near the track. The lady in the blue velvet bonnet twisted her gloves and twittered, but everyone else seemed to take the alarming ride in high good spirits.

It was almost ten o'clock on the dot when the cars coasted into the Hollidaysburg canal basin. The town itself was dark, with only a window here and there showing the gleam of lamplight. The freight boats moored in the warehouse slips were dark, too, for their hard-working crews would be up before dawn. Only at the packet slip were there lanterns and signs of life. Several coaches were drawn up on the town side of the tracks, waiting to take the passengers off to Moore's Hotel for the night.

"Dear me, so many gentlemen!" fluttered the lady in the blue velvet bonnet as she peered out through her window. There were certainly more figures waiting on the wharf than could be coach drivers.

"Perhaps they are a deputation here to meet someone," suggested an elderly woman.

Several passengers cast sideways glances at the man in the fur-collared brown coat. He looked important enough to deserve a welcoming committee, but he was clearly as curious as the others, for he raised his window and leaned out for a better view. Sam and Cherry followed his example.

"Look! There's Mam and Pap!"

Captain Dobbs, carrying one of the *Betty D.*'s lanterns, strode along the wharf toward the waiting group of men, with Mrs. Dobbs, Merry, and Darsie trotting to keep up.

Cherry scrambled for the front door of the car. Sam closed the window and caught up to her out on the platform.

"Miss Dobbs? Master Dobbs?" An eager, stout man with fuzzy side whiskers and a checked waistcoat bustled forward. "If I may introduce myself, I am Dudley Buncombe, editor of the *Hollidaysburg Gazette*—and I believe this is yours, Miss Dobbs?"

He handed up to Cherry a familiar notebook with a torn cover. Cherry, speechless, could only blink and hug Summer Moon's stories to her chest.

As the rest of the Dobbses came up, the newspaperman indicated a tall man in an old-fashioned, low-crowned hat and handsome gray mustache, and beyond him Sheriff Jackson from Mount Union. Philadelphia Smeal had joined them, and Parson Golightly was there, and so, too—in manacles and leg-irons—were Sim Owlglass and Perk Meago.

"By jingo, you caught 'em!" Sam crowed.

Mr. Smeal hooked his thumbs in his suspenders and grinned. "They figgered they'd best not come down the mountain the same way they went up. I spotted 'em slippin' out of a freight car a ways up from the foot of number ten. There was four of us at the hitchin' station, and only two o' them."

Sheriff Jackson beamed. "I rode over soon as the word

150

came. It may be we can give 'em scarcely a rap on the knuckles for takin' your book there, but I aim to cart 'em back to Dauphin County to stand trial for all the horse stealin'. Over there they have a nice, tight new jail that'll keep 'em out of our hair for a good spell."

"You young people have had a grand day," Mr. Buncombe said, "and I mean to write an account of it for the *Gazette* if we may have a word or two with you tomorrow. But I have a confession to make as well. Miss Dobbs, I have read your lively stories. They are unpolished, perhaps, but—such zest! If it is agreeable to you, I would like to print one or two in our newspaper."

"Well, I swow!" exclaimed Captain Dobbs.

"Jiminy!" said Sam.

"Jiminy!" Cherry echoed in a whisper.

18

And Afterward

The Dobbses—except for Baby Ellen—stayed up very late indeed, first to hear every detail of Cherry and Sam's adventure and then, because even with the children tucked up in bed no one could settle down to sleep, they settled down instead to hear Mrs. Dobbs read the fifth chapter of Mr. Dickens's *Nicholas Nickleby*.

Darsie's eyes grew round as Schoolmaster Squeers cruelly teased the little boys and picked his teeth with his fork, but it was not long before his eyes grew heavy and he burrowed under the covers.

Merry bit her lip to think of Nicholas having to go off with horrid Mr. Squeers to teach at his horrid school, but though she fought against it, she was asleep before their coach left for Yorkshire.

Sam lasted until the Yorkshire coach stopped to take on a passenger in Islington, but then slid into a dream of wheels and gears and whistles, and himself an engineer driving a large and shiny steam engine over a mile-high bridge.

Cherry lasted until almost the end of the chapter, when the coach turned over in a snowstorm and pitched Nicholas into the road. As Mrs. Dobbs closed the book, Captain Dobbs leaned over Cherry to pull her blanket up and saw that she was smiling.

She was dreaming of a bookshop with tall shelves and shining lamps, and gleaming oak tables piled high with copies of *The Indian Maid's Revenge*. In embossed covers. With gold lettering.

And Mr. Charles Dickens was buying a copy.